I Wish You Love

ALICE'S STORY

TUCKAWAY BAY
BOOK FIVE

MADELEINE JAIMES

SAND DUNE BOOKS

Sand Dune Books by Maddie James

www.maddiejamesbooks.com

Author: Jaimes, Madeleine

Title: I Wish You Love: Alice's Story / Madeleine Jaimes

Description: First edition. Sand Dune Books

Identifiers: eBook ISBN: 978-1-62237-568-4, Trade Paperback ISBN: 978-1-62237-569-1

Subjects: Fiction / Women's Fiction | Friendships | Relationships| Family | Saga | Beach Book

Creative Work & Design by Jacobs Ink, LLC

Published by Turquoise Morning, LLC., dba Jacobs Ink, LLC.

PO Box 20, New Holland, OH 43145.

Learn more about Madeleine Jaimes at www.maddiejamesbooks.com

Join the VIP Newsletter List at https://maddiejamesbooks.com/pages/newsletter

I Wish You Love

Had she waited years for the perfect moment that would never come?

Alice McBain spent a lifetime putting others first—her family, her friends, and Marilyn Morgan, the woman she's secretly loved for over a decade.

But Marilyn isn't just the mayor of Tuckaway Bay and Alice's superior—she's running for a state Senate seat and insists on keeping their relationship under wraps until after the election. Her constituents, and her husband, must never know.

Even though Alice has come to an amicable arrangement with her own husband, she is tired of hiding. After years of whispers and waiting, she wants the life she and Marilyn have dreamed of for years—out loud and in the open.

But when she finally finds the courage to demand more than hidden moments, the carefully constructed façade of her life crumbles. The fallout touches everything. Her family is thrown into chaos, and Marilyn's political ambitions hang in the balance.

And the woman who's always put others first must decide what love truly means when you finally choose yourself.

I Wish You Love is poignant, powerful story of identity, sacrifice, and the courage to live—and love—authentically.

From The Christmas Storm...

The thing that happened between Carol Oliver and Ella McBain at Sea Glass Inn.

"Okay, ladies. Look. We're stuck here—in this restaurant, inside this hotel, in the middle of this Christmas storm—so let's make the best of it. We're not chasing boy toys, and we're going to get along. Right? No drama." Hannah Watters scowled at the group.

Carol Oliver narrowed her gaze, first glancing at Ella McBain— sweet, smart, always the good girl, Ella—and then at Hannah, whom she hadn't quite nailed yet, personality-wise. She was sort of bossy, though. "Girl, drama is my middle name," she said.

"See?" Ella said. "You *are* just like your mother. I swear, Maggie Oliver keeps my mother spun up into a tizzy most of the time."

"Well, maybe Alice McBain needs to keep her nose out of *my* mother's business."

"And perhaps *your* mother," Ella shot back, "should figure out her life so *my* mother doesn't have to worry. I mean, she and Lia and Julia are always anxious about everything going on between her and your dad. And whether or not you realize it, you are just like her—helpless, vulnerable, gullible, and self-centered."

For a moment, Carol was kind of shocked, speechless even. *How fucking dare her? What do they know about my mom and dad?* Then Ella's last words hit her, and the heat of anger flushed up her neck to her cheeks. She pushed at Hannah. "Let me out."

Hannah braced herself against the table. "Wait."

"Why? I don't need to stay here and be insulted."

Ella leaned forward. "Sit back, Carol. What are you going to do, anyway? There's nothing going on. The Sandcastle Restaurant is the only place where anything is happening. In fact, I may just sit here until lunch, and then dinner."

"Well, that's an exciting life." Carol rolled her eyes, shifting her gaze toward the hot guy again.

"That's me. Boring Ella."

"Just like your mom," Carol bit back. "Boring, mother hen, Alice."

Ella shot Carol a look. "Why do you say that?"

"Because that's what my mom always says. In fact, she makes fun of your mom behind her back because she's such a goody-two-shoes."

Hannah laughed. "I haven't heard that phrase since I was a kid."

Ella stood up. "And your mother screws any guy in a pickup truck who is the opposite of your dad!"

"Whoa." Hannah shot daggers at Ella. "That's a lot uncalled for."

"She does not!" Carol batted at Hannah. "Let me out now."

Hannah pushed out of the booth.

Carol passed.

Ella stomped off toward the restroom and Hannah followed.

Oh, no you don't. Within seconds, Carol caught up with Ella in the hallway, grabbed her arm, swung her around, and stood nose-to-nose with her. "And your mother is a...a...."

Ella stood her ground. "A what? Cat got your tongue? Hard to find anything to pin on my mom since she's such a goody-two-shoes?"

Carol wanted to blast her. Ella was always so...good. She was an honor student, or so her mother said. And she was pretty and popu-lar. Her mother reminded her of that often. *Why can't you be more like Ella?* She would say. Ella never got into trouble at school, and she was going to college on an academic scholarship.

"*Your* mother...."

"Yes?"

Carol took another step and peered into Ella's perfect blue eyes. "Your mother humps women. She's a lesbian, and she's been hiding it from you for years. So how about that? Think she's perfect now?"

One

Alice McBain faced the seaside motel and smiled. It wasn't often that she and Marilyn could finagle a getaway for an entire weekend, but this was a celebration, of sorts. The May primary was over, and Marilyn had one more hurdle to cross before taking the North Carolina capitol by storm.

Winning the primary wasn't the only thing that made her giddy—winning meant they were one step closer to their happily-ever-after goal. They'd planned it for far too long. Perhaps things were finally coming together.

She retrieved her bag from the trunk, glancing past the old building to the ocean. The Buxton Motel had been a mainstay for tourists and anglers on the island for decades, but they'd never been there. She and Marilyn rarely stayed in the Outer Banks, opting for Virginia Beach or Norfolk, where they could get lost in the crowds. But with the madness leading up to the primary, she didn't have time to plan a trip north. Plus, if Marilyn had lost the primary race, there would be no celebration.

So, Alice, who always made their reservations and planned their itineraries, waited until the last minute to plan a getaway. Luckily, since the summer tourist season hadn't yet kicked in, the motel on Hatteras Island, an hour south of Tuckaway Bay, had vacancies.

And to Alice, that meant there wouldn't be many people. Of course, they probably wouldn't leave the room much, anyway.

After a quick check-in at the office, she carried her bag up to the second floor, where she located their oceanfront suite and unlocked the door. Her plan was simple. She'd drop off her things, then head to the local grocery store for water, goodies, and hopefully, something alcoholic. Afterward, she would set the stage and wait for the love of her life.

The door swung open, and she stepped inside. It wasn't the Ritz, not even a Marriott, but it was perfect—quaint, quiet, and since it was an end unit on the top floor, sinfully secluded.

She quickly texted Marilyn.

Alice: *I'm here. It's great.*

Marilyn: *I'm here too.*

What? Alice glanced at her watch. No.

Alice: *You're two hours early!*

Marilyn: *Ditched the budget meeting. Fuck 'em. What room?*

Alice: *Second floor. Facing ocean #22 on the end.*

Marilyn: *Can't wait.*

Shit! She'd wanted champagne on ice, and the mood set with music and flowers and chocolates. And....

Someone rapped on the door. "Alice? Sweetheart?"

Oh, well. She moved quickly to unlatch the door. Marilyn pushed inside the room, tossed her bag into a corner, and embraced her like she'd not seen her in years.

The kiss was deep and passionate, heating her cheeks and causing her breath to go shallow. Marilyn held her close, their bodies aligned. Despite feeling warm, Alice shivered as Marilyn brought her hands to her face and held her steady, while tracing her lips with her tongue. She fell limp under her caresses, opening her mouth to let her explore deeper.

Abruptly, Marilyn pushed her backwards toward the bed.

They tumbled into it with a burst of giggles.

"We. Are. Finally. Alone." Marilyn whispered the words, with a deliberate pause between each one, her breath feathering over Alice's face.

"Finally." Alice sighed, looking into her lover's eyes. "God, I love you."

Marilyn grinned and started undoing Alice's blouse, taking her lazy time with each button while she peered into her eyes.

Her body zinged with anticipation.

Get on with it. You're driving me crazy.

ALICE WOKE EARLY, ALONE IN THE BED. SHE LAY THERE FOR a moment, savoring the quiet, listening to the ocean, the rolling waves nearly lulling her back to sleep. That would not happen. She knew where Marilyn was. Rising, she wrapped her robe tight around her naked body and slipped out the door to the deck.

There.

Coffee mug in hand, Marilyn stared out over the ocean, waiting for the sunrise. Glancing over the horizon, Alice knew the yellow-orange orb would pop over the vista any second. It was that close. A soft saltwater breeze wafted over the deck, blowing Marilyn's shoulder-length, dark blond hair around her pretty face.

She never tired of watching her. That first glimpse always made her heart flutter.

Drawn to Marilyn from the moment their eyes met at Bayside Realty, over a dozen years ago, Alice never tired of how she felt when they were together. Back then, she couldn't put words to her feelings, or the attraction—until Marilyn started pursuing her, which had totally flabbergasted Alice.

She'd avoided contact with her for weeks, initially, until she couldn't.

She wasn't attracted to women. She was married—to a man, of course. Happily married. She didn't have affairs, and she didn't flirt. Her family, her marriage, meant everything. And George, her husband, was extremely loyal and nothing shy of perfect. He was a great dad, a devoted and doting husband, and in every sense of the word, her partner.

No. She wasn't gay, or a lesbian. Or bisexual.

Was she?

That day, standing in the lobby of the rental agency, when their gazes had locked and held, Alice suddenly wasn't sure of anything any longer. Unexpected things were happening with her body that had never happened before with a woman.

Thrilling things.

Sexual things.

Indescribable things.

Disturbing things.

And yes, she'd been ashamed, until Marilyn ultimately convinced her that what she felt was normal and okay—but that had taken time.

"You're up." Marilyn's soft words came to her on the breeze.

Alice realized she'd been staring past her toward the ocean, lost in thought. Lost in the wonder of the years they'd shared since they met. "I am. The bed was cold. I missed you."

Marilyn's wisp of a smile made her heart sing a little. She was happy.

They were both happy.

"This coffee is so bad."

Marilyn's words jerked Alice out of her musing, and she laughed. "I'm sure it's terrible."

"But the sunrise is... Splendid."

Stepping closer, Alice slipped her arm around Marilyn's waist, laying her head on her shoulder. "So peaceful."

"Yes."

"We needed this."

Marilyn set her coffee mug on the deck railing and cupped Alice's cheek in her cool hand. "Yes, we did, my darling. I know the past few months have not been easy on you."

"Or you."

"Oh, I thrive on the madness. You, on the other hand, tolerate it." She brushed her lips across hers. "And I thank you every single day. You know I couldn't have won the primary, or endured my years as mayor, without you." Her gaze penetrated, and then she whispered. "You are my rock, darling. My one and only."

Alice smiled back. "I'd walk ten thousand miles through crazy madness knowing you were waiting on the other side."

Marilyn brushed a few hairs back from her forehead, her fingertips softly skimming Alice's skin, and peered into her eyes. "Ten thousand miles is excessive, don't you think? Let's just get through November, and then we can finally make plans for our future."

Alice's chest swelled with happiness. "Promise?"

"Promise."

Marilyn was rarely the one to bring up their future. Alice had resigned herself to that fact over the years. So, hearing her say those words, feeling the depth of their meaning in her heart as her lover stared into her eyes, made Alice's entire weekend.

Marilyn's gaze held firm, and Alice could tell she was thinking about something.

"What is it?" she asked

A soft sigh escaped her lips, and she locked her arms around Alice's back. "Sweetheart, the next few months are going to be insane. I hope you realize what you've signed on for—campaign manager and all. I fear we may have to stretch to find alone time from here on out."

"I realize that. But it's for the greater good. Right?

She flashed a wide smile. "Exactly. So, let's enjoy today and tomorrow. All hell breaks loose on Monday."

"It's a plan."

Marilyn brushed her lips across Alice's. "And in December? We make up for lost time," she whispered.

Her kiss deepened, and Alice grasped the lapels of her robe and pulled her closer.

Lost time. She'd waited nearly fourteen years for Marilyn. Was their future finally within their grasp?

Two

A month later, Alice stepped into her office, frowning at the mess on her desk.

A stack of folders leaned haphazardly against her desktop organizer. Campaign flyers poked out of a drawer. Two paper cups, half full of cold coffee, stood precariously perched near the edge of the desk mat. Her planner lay open, showing last week's dates. Pens were scattered over everything, and a box of paperclips had apparently exploded by her desktop computer.

She had to move those flyers soon. Marilyn had warned her against having political materials anywhere near the mayor's office. It was the town council ethics committee policy—no campaign work or discussion of ongoing campaigns in any government office.

No exception.

Ever.

They'd already violated that—had pushed the envelope on those local regulations—more than once, and that seriously went against her grain. Everyone knew that Alice McBain was the *goody-two-shoes, mother-hen-protector, fixer-of-everything, follow-the-rules* kind of girl.

But she *was* following Marilyn's orders.

And the last thing she wanted was to make Marilyn unhappy or upset about anything right now. Hopefully, her boss would be in a good mood today. While the town hall event last evening went long, the feedback coming in this morning was tremendous, encouraging, and positive. She supposed it was worth being run ragged all week, given that the town hall launched the upcoming summer campaign tour.

While Marilyn was typically an organized, pulled-together woman, lately she'd been barking haphazard orders like a drill sergeant on crack.

Get a grip, Alice.

But the ugly mess on her desk seriously rivaled the mess in her head.

In her life.

And this commotion wasn't likely to go away anytime soon. It was late June. Four more months, roughly, until the November election. They were currently staffing up to get a jump on the August-to-October political push.

As if the election were the only thing causing her stress....

However, this clutter was so unlike her, and she needed to rectify the situation sooner rather than later. She liked things neat and orderly. Craved that, actually. *A place for everything and everything in its place.* Isn't that how the saying goes? That was her, for sure. She rarely left her workspace without tidying up, shutting down her computer, and dusting off her desk.

Admit it, Alice. Your life went from perfect to shit in about three-point-five seconds. Or, to be more accurate, since the Christmas storm at Sea Glass Inn several months ago where your dirty laundry was aired for all to see—and judge.

Marilyn burst through the door—one consequence of having an office connected to your boss's—and Alice jerked her head up.

"Oh, you're here," she said. "I checked a minute ago, and you hadn't arrived yet." She glanced at her watch. Marilyn insisted on staff punctuality, and far be it from her to grant Alice any slack. When they were at the office, she was just another staff member.

Alice reached to her left and grabbed a fresh to-go cup of coffee and handed it to her. "Your morning coffee. Dark, hot, and devoid of anything pleasurable." She smiled.

Marilyn blinked, shook her head, and grinned. "You're a lifesaver. I didn't have time to stop this morning."

Alice shrugged. "I figured. The event went late, and I knew you'd sleep until the last minute."

"I have a meeting with Callahan in..." Marilyn glanced at her watch. "Three minutes. The coffee is perfect. Thanks."

"Is this about the dune revitalization grant?"

David Callahan, the city manager—who worked closely with Marilyn daily—was continually searching for new funding for town and beach improvements. He'd be a likely candidate for mayor if Marilyn landed the state Senate seat in the fall. Marilyn had been grooming him for the potential likelihood that he could step into her shoes if elected. Of course, Callahan insisted he was nonpolitical and had no interest in running.

Marilyn did not let that deter her.

She nodded and stared at Alice's desk, like it was the first time she'd noticed the mess. "It is the dune grant. Yes."

"I'll get this cleaned up while you're gone."

"I was surprised to see it when I got here. Not like you, Alice."

"I know." She started scooping up paper clips. "We left in a hurry yesterday. Remember?"

Again, another nod from Marilyn. "We did. But your office is the gateway to the Mayor's office—*my office*—and appearances are important. Right? We can't have people going around talking about us running a sloppy office, and me running a messy town."

"No, you're right. Of course."

"Plus, this looks like a campaign headquarters, not a mayor's reception area. We talked about that." She glanced about.

"Yes."

"We're pushing it here. Since we're ramping up for the summer, it's time to get a headquarters set up somewhere away from this office. Get on that today."

Alice nodded. "Definitely."

"And hire that kid who volunteered at the town hall last night.

The young man who helped us with all the tech stuff and other logistics."

"Matthew Miller?" Matt was a local, just graduated from Duke with an undergraduate degree in political science. While Alice knew he was starting grad school in the fall, he appeared competent and eager to step into the political arena. Maybe it could work.

"Yes. Hire him. He can run the office under your direction." More barked orders. Split-second decisions made.

Though, hiring Matt *could* be a lifesaver. Alice had wondered how much longer she could effectively do two jobs—Marilyn's campaign manager and assistant to the mayor. "Of course. I'll call him ASAP."

"Clean up this crap first."

"Right, Marilyn. I'm on it. All of it."

Marilyn stared for a few seconds, holding Alice's gaze. "I have to go. Callahan is a stickler for promptness." She smirked and leaned closer, her cool, gray-eyed gaze penetrating. At her side, Marilyn reached for her hand and tangled their fingers together.

Alice shivered a little, suddenly craving their closeness. It had been a while since Hatteras. A month. So many things in the way.

Marilyn covertly glanced at the closed outer office door and gave her a quick peck on the lips.

Alice hated how needy she felt at that moment.

"I think we need a campaign strategy dinner meeting tonight," she whispered. "Don't you?"

With a sigh, she agreed. "Yes."

Marilyn stepped back and tossed her a promising grin. "We'll discuss details later."

"David values promptness."

A wide grin stretched across Marilyn's face. "Precisely why I'm making him wait."

Of course. Because you're the one in charge, my sweet Marilyn.

Alice smiled and watched her leave. No wonder she'd fallen in love with the woman all those years ago. She was everything Alice wasn't. The other half of her psyche. The id to her ego. The yin to her yang. The Alpha to her beta.

The Dom to her sub.

God help her.

BAYSIDE REALTY, FOURTEEN YEARS EARLIER

"DAMMIT."

Hazelnut coffee sloshed over the side of Alice's cup and onto the back of her hand. Another day starting off like horses from the gate, and with a headache.

She set the cup on her desk, shook coffee off her hand, and reached for a tissue. Wiping off the drips, she then tossed the tissue in the small trash can under her desk and reached for her day calendar. Flipping the planner open with one hand, she typed in her four-digit passcode with the other, bringing her desktop computer to life.

The voicemail button on her phone blinked steadily.

While listening to the messages, she jotted down notes on a sticky pad, while monitoring the stack of emails sliding into her inbox and scanning today's to-do list. With the voice messages finished, she glanced at the upbeat "quote of the day" on the planner page and chuckled, remembering how excited she'd been when she'd chosen that organizer.

Uplifting and inspiring. *Sheesh*. She barely had time to read them.

However, within two minutes, Alice had gotten a handle on her day and identified the immediate fires to put out. Let the multitasking begin.

Slightly overwhelmed, she rubbed her temple, looking up as Marilyn Morgan—the newly hired agent at Bayside Realty—stepped into the lobby from her office down the hall. Alice hadn't realized anyone else was there.

Her job as office manager meant she kept the business humming along during the day. Her workspace in the lobby corner was comprised of a high counter wrapped around her L-shaped desk. She could look up and over when clients arrived, welcoming them to the agency. On top of the counter, she had placed business cards for all the agents, a sign-in sheet for their email newsletter, a bowl of hard candies—wrapped, of course—and a stack of refrigerator magnets with their logo and phone number, and their yearly calendar.

Chairs for clients lined the front wall, on either side of the door. End tables held magazines. The coffee table provided a portfolio of current housing offerings. Beachy pictures and other beach-vibe knickknacks completed the space. Alice was proud of how it looked. When hired, her supervisor provided a budget for decorating the lobby. She'd nailed it, or so she was told.

The space was warm, cozy, and made her feel happy and comfortable.

"It's too early in the day for a headache."

Alice reached for her coffee cup and took a sip. "Not enough caffeine yet."

The new agent strode quietly into her space and toward the desk, one high-heeled foot in front of the other—one slow, but determined, step at a time.

They locked gazes briefly until Alice dropped hers and looked away. "It's spring. Allergies."

"I see." Marilyn paused alongside her desk.

Suddenly, Alice was uncomfortable in her space. And the weird thing was, she didn't know why. At first.

Slowly, she lifted her chin. Marilyn's filmy blouse was unbuttoned low enough to reveal a subtle hint of cleavage, the lavender fabric tucked into a silver-gray pencil skirt. Alice imagined there was a jacket to match that skirt hanging from the hanger on a hook behind her office door. An opaque set of pearls circled her neck and flowed over the rise of her breasts.

Eventually, her eyes met Marilyn's again.

"Good morning." *Stupid.* She should have said that earlier. Her throat felt tight, so she took another drink of coffee. "What can I do for you?"

Marilyn set a stack of files on the desk. "I'm unfamiliar with the office protocol. Do you file these in the main file? Or should I? They are older listings."

"Oh, please." Alice took them. "I'll file them. I have a system."

Smiling, Marilyn held her gaze. "Also, I have a couple of new listings to upload online." She leaned closer as she handed her another file.

Alice got a good look at the further exposed cleavage, and a hint of a black lacy bra.

"Can you edit the descriptions first though? And run them by me before you upload?"

"Uh...of course." She risked a glance up, her gaze skimming Marilyn's eyes. "Yes, that's what I do."

Alice fiddled with her coffee cup, trying to get a grip on it.

Slowly, Marilyn placed her hand over Alice's, stopping her from picking up the cup. "You really should slow down on the caffeine, *Alice*," she said softly. "I think it's making you a little jittery."

No. No. That's not it.

She was confused, not jittery, and it wasn't the coffee. It wasn't the first time Marilyn had made her nervous.

"Alice?"

It's your touch. Your presence. Your soft hand resting on mine. Your plum-painted nails, manicured fingers...possessing, caressing, my knuckles. Jumbling my thoughts.

I like your hand there.

And I like the way my name rolls off your tongue.

And I have no business liking any of that.

Alice withdrew her hand and buried it in her lap. "I'm fine, Marilyn. I'll take care of those files and get back to you about the descriptions later today." She dragged the stack of files closer.

Marilyn stood over her for several more seconds.

Will she not leave?

Alice glanced up, catching Marilyn's gaze. Or perhaps, Marilyn caught hers.

"I'll look forward to that."

She left, and Alice collapsed back into her chair and exhaled. Had she been holding her breath? Her hand still shook.

Dammit.

By the time Marilyn's meeting with Callahan was over, Alice had cleaned her office and tidied up Marilyn's too. She'd been working for the woman for a long time, so she knew exactly what to do, and what not to do—what items to touch and move, and which items to leave alone. She'd only suffered Marilyn's wrath once, not long after they'd first met.

When they'd worked together at Bayside—a small agency dealing with vacation and residential home sales—most agents, including Marilyn, left by five o'clock. Alice didn't leave until five-thirty. While a cleaning service came once a week, it was part of Alice's job description to see that the lobby and offices were kept clean in between. That gave her thirty minutes with no one around to do the quick dusting in the four agent offices, plus the lobby and outer office, which was her domain. There were days some agents didn't come into the office at all, and she could dust earlier. Win-win.

So, she knew the drill. She'd known exactly what Marilyn was referring to earlier that morning when she'd said she didn't want to give the impression to the public that she ran a sloppy government office.

Marilyn was all about appearance and perception. If the public perceived something to be true, then it was. *If what they believe is to our advantage*, she would say, *then lean into it. If it's detrimental to our cause, then spin it until we own it.*

That was her attitude, basically, in work, play, and life.

Not a local, Marilyn had moved into the area the year before she'd started at Bayside, when her husband became the general manager of a local construction firm. And since vacation businesses—accommodations, retail, rentals and leasing, restaurants, and the like—were the backbone of the Outer Banks economy, the construction business boomed.

The same could be said, back then, for real estate—and the town of Tuckaway Bay was no exception to that rule. Growth was steady and imminent for the foreseeable future.

Marilyn had rapidly proved herself as a top-selling agent. She burst onto the scene like a hurricane and left a definite trail of destruction and wonder in her wake. Never intimidated, she kowtowed to no one, and played the business like it was her fiddle.

It didn't take her long to become well known in the coastal town of Tuckaway Bay.

Alice had admired that...and her. Marilyn won local and regional awards and eventually made quite a name for herself in the real estate arena across the state. There were even billboards with her picture sprinkled up and down the major highways. Anyone thinking of buying a house at the beach knew Marilyn was *the* agent to call.

The woman was on top of everything. In control. Assertive, direct, and always right. And if she wasn't, she faked it. Her hunches about buyers, and whether they would bite, were spot on. Her predictions about sales trends and markets were constantly on point.

She knew her game and was a master at dominating the field.

And in the political world, she was even better.

Alternatively, Alice was the invisible person in the room at Bayside. While she knew then that she'd seamlessly kept things running and in tip-top shape, if she were to have unexpectedly not shown up one day, all hell would break loose.

She was the coffee maker, phone answerer, copy machine fixer, appointment maker, meeting planner, paper filer, contracts drafter, listing copy editor and uploader, marketer, supply orderer, database owner, budget tracker, notary, and customer service provider.

She got things done quietly and without fanfare. And as long as tasks were done well and correctly, she remained unseen—there and present, but mostly ignored, until someone needed something. That's when she jumped and delivered without question.

That's why she'd let her guard down, somewhat, when Marilyn—who had been there less than a month at that point—had called after a showing and asked her to tidy up her desk early that afternoon. She had a late client meeting at five.

So, Alice did. She'd wanted to make sure everything was perfect for this woman who had overtaken her thoughts, invaded her fantasies, and made her sizzle every time she got close. She'd dusted and organized the office, emptied half-full coffee cups, and took them to the kitchenette to wash. She'd emptied the small trash can under her desk and made sure Marilyn had fresh yellow legal pads—her preferred vessel for note-taking—in her desk drawer, along with her favorite pens.

While in the kitchenette, Alice made a fresh pot of coffee for the thermos carafe, retrieved two more clean coffee cups and containers of cream, sugar, and sweetener arranged on a tray. She set it all up neatly on the cabinet behind Marilyn's desk.

As she left her office, Alice glanced at the stack of files and Marilyn's open day planner. She closed the planner and straightened it on the desktop. Standing back, she admired her handiwork. The workspace was organized and ready for a meeting.

Except for those damn files. Did Marilyn really want those there?

With little thought, she lifted the stack, rifled through it, and realized they were all old client files from previously sold properties. Marilyn had her file a similar stack the week before, hadn't she? She couldn't imagine she'd need them today, as these listings were all wrapped up and closed.

So, she took them back to her office and filed them in the main filing system. Once she'd done all that, she left for home.

Three

"Yes. Yes. That sounds perfect."

An hour later, Alice was on the phone with the owner of a potential office rental downtown, when Marilyn breezed through her space, crossed the room without eye contact, and slipped into the mayor's office.

The older gentleman on the other end of the line rambled on.

She gave the door a quick glance, turning slightly in her seat to see if Marilyn had shut it, then returned her attention to the caller. "That price may be doable if it includes utilities," she told him. "Am I correct in assuming it does?"

"Well, now. Not usually...."

"I see. We do have other options that might better suit our budget then, although your space is the perfect location. I understand it's been empty for some time, though. Correct?"

The older gentleman hemmed and hawed for a moment, then reneged. "Fine. Utilities included. But if the water bill goes over a hundred dollars a month, I'm billing for overage."

"Great. I'd like to see the space this week, if possible."

They continued their chat and agreed on a two o'clock walk-through the next afternoon. Alice hung up and jotted down the meeting time in her planner. Just as she was entering the appointment in her personal online calendar—so Marilyn could see it if she chose to—her phone buzzed with a text message.

Marilyn: *Come here when off call.*

Alice: *Be right there.*

Marilyn always texted. She despised the office intercom system, saying she didn't like anyone in the outer office hearing her requests. Texting just worked better.

Alice pushed open the door to Marilyn's office and caught her expression as she stood, hands on hips, behind her desk. She looked up sharply as Alice entered.

"My tablet is gone." Her gaze was intense.

"No, it's not. It's in the middle drawer on the right."

Marilyn huffed, then bent to pull out the drawer. She retrieved the tablet and then frowned.

"You know I like it on my desk. Not in the drawer. I want things where I want them."

Alice bit her lip, then said exactly what was on her mind. "Of course. I learned that lesson years ago."

Marilyn stared daggers. "Good God, Alice. You need to let that go. What's it been? Twelve years? Thirteen?"

"Fourteen, actually."

"Jesus. I can't believe you know exactly how long."

Alice held Marilyn's gaze. "There are some things you don't easily forget. Like, humiliation."

Marilyn blew out a breath and momentarily closed her eyes. "I apologized then. I was out of line. And I suppose I'll be apologizing for the rest of my life—but you never should have removed those files."

"They were closed files."

"I was researching past sales. And we've been over this a thousand times."

"You were mean. I almost quit my job that day."

Marilyn threw up her hands. "Yes, I yelled at you. And I chose the wrong time to do it. I'm fucking sorry, Alice. Give it a rest."

She should, she supposed, *give it a fucking rest*, but even though

Alice loved the woman to no end, there were times she wanted her to know just exactly how much she had hurt her that day, fourteen years ago, when she'd had a meltdown in the outer office in front of all the agents, and some clients waiting in the lobby.

It still stung. Especially when Marilyn was being pissy, like today.

Alice had then, and still felt, embarrassed every time Marilyn was ridiculously trivial and picky about how she'd done something.

"Well, just keep the tablet on the desk. Don't move things if I have them there."

"Right. This week, you mean."

"What?"

"Last week you wanted it in the drawer."

Marilyn's eyes grew larger. "Okay then. Well. This week I want the goddamn tablet on my desk. Right beside my goddamn planner."

Alice studied her. "Alright."

After a moment, Marilyn sat. Alice remained standing.

"What?" she asked.

Might as well jump on in, Miss Fix-it. "You're super erratic these past few days. I know it's a stressful time. Not only your job but with the campaign ramping up. What can I take off your plate?" Alice always found it helpful, and to her advantage, if she acknowledged the situation and put a name to it—even if Marilyn wouldn't or couldn't—and then offered some sort of solution.

In fact, she never went to her *boss-slash-lover* with any problem unless she had ideas to solve it. Marilyn might not agree with her, but at the very least, they started a dialogue about the issue.

Marilyn sighed and studied her, her features softening. "God, I'm sorry. You're right, as always. I am stressed to the max and very much in need of dinner with you tonight. That's what you can do for me."

Alice grew warm just thinking about it. "Shall I make reservations?"

"Please." Marilyn opened her laptop.

She smiled. "I'll double-check our schedules. Should I call Jonathan and let him know you are working late tonight?" There were days Alice communicated more with Marilyn's husband than she did.

Marilyn pushed out another sigh. "No, I'll do it. You handle

George. I know he's been on the questionable side of late. But thanks."

Alice nodded and sat across from her, the desk between them. George wouldn't be an issue. He never questioned where she was going or who she was with, especially if it was work or campaign related. He *knew* who she was with and tolerated it. And he knew who Marilyn was to her.

But at that moment, their husbands weren't what worried Alice.

While Marilyn had her days—more frequently, lately, because of the campaign stress—and could be grouchy as hell when she was tired and frustrated, today was different.

Something was different. "Tell me."

"Well, shit. You see too much." Marilyn fiddled with the computer mouse, taking a moment and staring at the screen. "I should know by now that I can't keep things from you."

"Something happened. What?"

"Callahan didn't want to meet about the grant."

"Oh?"

She leaned forward. "No. He resigned."

Oh, shit. "What? No."

Marilyn nodded. "Precisely my reaction. On top of everything else, we need to either hire or appoint a new city manager ASAP. He's leaving in two weeks."

"Appointing someone internally will be quicker. Maybe an interim? But doesn't the city council have to weigh in on this? Conducting a search will take time."

"Time we do not have. Time *I* don't have—I can't take on his responsibilities, in addition to mine, right now."

"Exactly." Alice bit her lip. "I can get right on it. I'll make a list of potential internal candidates, then get with Connie over in H.R. and pull the latest job description. We might want to update that and...."

"Stop." Marilyn stood, shaking her head. "No. Let me mull this over for a few hours. You're right. The council hires the city manager and probably they will want to cast a wide net and conduct a search. We need to be ready for that and provide our input. Let's put our heads together over dinner. Seven at Winnie's, right?"

"Yes." Their usual place and time. "Of course. I'll call and confirm."

"Good." Marilyn cracked a smile.

Turning, Alice started to her office, then glanced back. "Marilyn, did David say why he is leaving?"

"Oh yes. And he wasn't shy about the details, either. He's going to work for Faust."

"Wait. What? Fred Faust's *campaign*?"

"Yes. Ironic, isn't it?"

All Alice could do was stare, dumbfounded. "Shit. You're kidding."

"Oh no. I'm not. Faust fired his communication director last week and offered David the position. Seems they are old college friends. I had no clue the man was even political. He *claims* he's nonpartisan. Plus, he's always been very middle-of-the-road in casual conversation." She drummed her fingers on the desktop and stared at Alice. "But I really thought I was getting through to him about running for mayor, if I win the election."

"*When* you win the election."

She met Alice's gaze. "It's going to be a tough fight. And now, maybe tougher."

"Right." It *was* curious. Alice blinked a few times, still holding Marilyn's gaze. "He was at the town hall last night, though. I was honestly glad to see him there, thinking we had his support."

"Apparently not. I questioned him about that, and he said he was simply there as a citizen. He claims he's a registered Independent, and that he took the position with Faust for the experience."

"Bullshit."

Marilyn smiled at her word choice. Alice didn't let a curse word fly often. "Exactly."

"Are you worried?"

She shrugged. "Seriously, Alice? My right-hand man just told me he's jumping ship to work for the enemy. Am I worried? I probably should be, but honestly, I need to mull that over, too."

"Understandable."

"Well, there's not much I can do about it now. Let's get on with our day."

"Sure." But it was worrisome. Alice turned and headed back to her office, thinking about this new situation. She softly closed the door behind her while mentally sifting through conversations with Callahan. What did he know? Had seen? What conversations had he been privy to, or overheard?

Hopefully, nothing of any significance. They'd been careful.

But David Callahan's leaving was potential trouble. She could smell it. He wasn't just working for the enemy now—he was working for Fred Faust, the conservative senatorial candidate running against Marilyn's liberal agenda.

Four

George McBain liked to think of himself as a simple man.

There were three things in life he held most dear—in fact, one might call them more than essential for his happiness—and those three things were all he needed.

Teaching.

Theater.

And his wife and daughter, Alice and Ella.

Not necessarily in that order of importance.

He was a born teacher and actor—the two had gone hand-in-hand throughout his education career. For twenty-two years he'd taught social studies and history at Tuckaway Bay Middle School to sixth-through-eighth grade students. With a college double major in Social Studies Education and Theater, he provided his students with rich dramatic renditions of historical events and current social situations right there in the classroom. He would dress the part, speak the part, be the part from the moment he stepped onto the school campus until he left for the day. He would entice his students to dramatize the events along with him.

Tuckaway Bay and the Outer Banks, was ripe with historical significance, which fueled his muse. From Virginia Dare and the

Roanoke Colony, to Blackbeard and the pirate era, to the Spanish mustangs, to Civil War and World War II battles and shipwrecks, and more, the area was mere fodder for his creative whimsy.

Parents, students, and the faculty and staff loved it. And while it was important to George that his students learned through the dramatic reenactments, that wasn't entirely his goal.

He did it because he loved it. Needed it. Because the theatrics of it all were a part of him.

During the summer months, when he was off school, he poured his efforts into working for The Lost Colony outdoor drama and had done so for over two decades. In the early years, he was part of the cast. Later he worked on sets, costumes, and occasionally in the ticket office. Wherever they needed him was fine—he simply enjoyed being part of the production.

THIS SUMMER, HE WAS FORTUNATE ENOUGH TO SNAG THE stage manager gig. He oversaw all the moving parts of the play—the shifting of sets, props, lighting, and such—ensuring that everything was in the right place at the right time. It was chaotic but also extremely rewarding.

He was headed there that evening.

"Dad? What are you fixing for dinner?"

If I can get out the door. George looked up from the kitchen island where he'd just sat a steaming hot covered dish. "How about tamale casserole fresh from the oven? Should probably let it cool first."

Ella leaned in and sniffed. "Yum. Did you put in very many peppers?"

"A few jalapeños, is all."

"Nothing hotter?"

"No." He smiled and nudged his daughter with his shoulder. "And I scraped the seeds. I know you're not a hot tamale."

Laughing, Ella winked. "That's not what the guys at school say."

George's heart skipped a beat. Ella was nineteen years old and had just finished her freshman year of college. She dated, of course. He knew that. And she'd probably been intimate with a boyfriend or two, maybe. He wasn't sure, and he'd never asked Alice if she knew because, frankly, he didn't want to know. Couldn't think of his baby girl doing...that.

He clutched at his chest. "You wound me, daughter. Say no more."

Ella laughed. "Good grief, Dad. The drama."

"I am drama, darling."

"But not the kind of drama people stir up. You're more like...*theater drama*."

He nodded. "I stand corrected. I do not like to stir up the shit."

Ella laughed. "The casserole looks great. I'll make a salad. When is Mom getting home?"

Who knows?

The subject of her mother was not one he often entertained with his daughter, especially the past few weeks since Ella was home from school. While he and Alice had covertly planned their divorce for a few years now, they had deliberately waited until Ella was settled into college life to act upon their plans.

That had been their intent. However, the chaos of Christmas had changed those plans abruptly when Carol Oliver had told the world— aka all their friends at Sea Glass Inn—that Alice was gay. Now, it seemed his little family was in perpetual limbo.

"Go ahead and eat," he said. "She's working late."

"But she has to eat. Let's take her a plate." Ella pulled lettuce and other vegetables from the refrigerator.

"She'll find something."

Ella turned and smiled. "But wouldn't it be nice to surprise her? She loves Tex-Mex foods, and this looks yummy." She turned back to the cabinet and pulled down a plastic container. "I'll fix it."

George stepped closer and took the container from her hands. "No. We're not taking her dinner."

"But why?"

Her big eyes were almost his undoing. He loved her without end. Alice, too. But sooner rather than later, Ella was going to have to face reality.

Hell. Who am I kidding? I have to face reality.

"She's having dinner with Marilyn after work. A campaign strategy meeting, apparently."

Ella simply stared. "Oh. I see."

"So, let's eat." There was no way he was going to rush out of here now. He could text his assistant to get things started. "I do have to leave in about an hour, though."

Ella blew out a breath. "Of course. The play."

He shrugged. "Well, it's summer."

"Right." She glanced at the vegetables. "I don't think I want a salad. Do you? In fact, I'm not really hungry after all. You eat and go. I'll heat something up later."

She turned away, but George caught her arm. "Ella?"

Halting, she faced him. "It's okay, Dad. I'm okay. Sometimes I forget things have changed. I guess..." She paused and shook her head.

"You guess what?"

"I guess while I was at school I didn't have to think about you and Mom splitting up. Or, about her and Marilyn. I still can't wrap my head around it. Can you?"

He couldn't. Never could, really. "No."

Squaring herself, she searched his eyes. "Then fix it. You can. Right? You've always been able to fix everything, Dad. Fix this with Mom so that we are a family again."

If only....

George shook his head. "Sweetheart, this may be one thing I can't fix."

"But you have to try. Right? I mean, it's us. You, me, and Mom. We've always been a team. And now...."

The look on Ella's face was one of desperation, and also concern, showing a certain vulnerability that was difficult to define. She wasn't a little girl anymore, but she suddenly looked like she was nine instead of nineteen. He wanted to sweep her up and hold her on his lap and cuddle away her troubles, like a skinned knee, or getting a B in her favorite class.

Not happening. He had to find another way to comfort her, but he wasn't sure he knew how. Ella had grown up. She was an adult. He had to face *that* reality, too.

"I don't know, baby girl. Maybe it's not my problem to fix."

"You're saying it's Mom's problem?"

He shook his head, grimacing. Alice didn't need fixing. She was who she was, as much as he didn't want to admit it. And could their marriage be fixed? Saved? It was doubtful.

She wanted something different now.

George stared into Ella's face, observing her expression. "I'm not saying that, Ella. Maybe what I'm saying is that your mom doesn't need fixing, she's fine the way she is, and no matter what, she's your mom. We respect her, and love her, and we should support her lifestyle, however she chooses to live it. It's just that we don't all fit together as a family like we used to. And maybe our marriage isn't fixable."

Ella said nothing for a moment, then turned and left the kitchen.

George covered the casserole with foil.

MARILYN WAS FIFTEEN MINUTES LATE.

Sitting at their table at Winnie's Wharf, Alice glanced again at her cell phone, as if the action would trigger a call or a text or something. Seven-sixteen. Nothing. Where the hell was she?

She didn't want to call because she knew Marilyn had gone home for about an hour after leaving work to discuss something with Jonathan. She wasn't sure what, because she'd not inquired or prodded Marilyn into telling her.

They didn't interfere in each other's lives with their husbands.

"I need to clear the air with him about something," she'd told Alice around five-thirty that evening. "Go home and connect with your family. I'll meet you at the restaurant."

Staring at the menu—not really seeing the words—Alice's mind drifted.

She hadn't wanted to go home. If she did, a discussion would likely happen—one she had been putting off for far too long. Since Ella was home for the summer, things had changed. She and George were used to navigating around each other and getting on with life.

They had separate bedrooms, didn't feel the need to keep tabs on each other, and came and went as they pleased. They no longer left notes for each other on the refrigerator.

But with Ella home, things were awkward again. While she and George had grown into their situation, Ella hadn't.

Of course, that was easily explained—this past semester, her child had barely come home, choosing to stay weekends on campus with her friends. Alice had thought it healthy for Ella. She needed to stretch her wings and grow into an independent being.

Now, she wondered if Ella was simply avoiding the home situation.

Out of sight, out of mind.

And in a way, hadn't she and George done that too? They'd said they would officially divorce after Ella was at ECU, but somehow, that didn't happen.

Fall had been busy.

Christmas and the New Year holiday were terribly awkward once Alice came out.

Was forced to come out. To her family and friends, anyway. Not publicly. Her girlfriends—Lia, Maggie, and Julia—had already known.

And since the primary, and the days after, she'd been totally immersed in the campaign. Their divorce had taken a backseat, and they had to remedy that soon.

"Alice? Goodness. I haven't seen you in ages."

Looking up, she saw an old friend from high school, Kathy Thacker, standing beside the table. "Kathy! Wow. It's been some time, I think."

"Too long!" She giggled, then Kathy waved to someone, motioning them closer. "Dean, come over here and see who I found. It's Alice McBain."

Oh dear. Dean Bryant. Shit. One of George's old friends. Alice stood. "Well, I'll be."

Dean moved in and hugged her. "So good to see you, Alice. Are you waiting for George?"

"No, I—"

"Oh! I hope so," Kathy interjected. "I just love George. In high school, you two were the cutest couple ever. So perfect. Always doting on each other. All the girls were jealous, you know."

She did know. The girls in her group consistently told her how lucky she was to have him.

Dean leaned closer and grasped her hands. "When he gets here, let's get a table together. We can rehash old times."

Alice pushed his hands away and released them. "Oh, I wish. That would be lovely, but actually, George is home tonight. I'm here for dinner with a friend. My boss, actually." She glanced from Kathy to Dean again, noticing Kathy's pouty face.

"Well, shoot," she said. "I don't get back here that often, but maybe the next time. Okay? I came to visit my mom, and Dean was in town, too. So, we decided to hang out."

Hang out? What are we? Teenagers?

She caught the twinkle in Kathy's eyes as she glanced at Dean and blushed. That's right. She had heard that Dean had divorced Cyndy Rollins, and Kathy's husband had passed a few years back.

Oh shit. They are dating.

"Definitely next time," she said. *Please go away now.* Alice dug in her purse and handed over a business card. "Here's my email and phone numbers. Give me a heads-up next time you're in town and I'll get us all together."

Again, Dean seized her hands. "Oh, please do, Alice. I would love to spend some time with the two of you. I've always admired your partnership."

Partnership. Yeah. Well, come back soon before all hell breaks loose.

Again, Alice let his hands go. The man was getting a little too forward. Besides, the last thing she needed right now was to be reminded of how perfect a couple she and George were. She glanced at the host stand. "Oh! I think they are looking for you."

Kathy's head whipped toward that area. "Yes!" She grasped Dean's arm. "Our table is ready, I think."

"Well, you two have fun."

"Will do!" Kathy gave Alice a quick kiss on the cheek. "Talk soon." She waved the business card as she and Dean trotted off toward the podium.

"Sure." Alice sat, suddenly exhausted, and gave her watch a peek. Seven-twenty-two.

"Hey. I'm here."

She glanced up.

Breathless, Marilyn tucked her bag onto an empty seat and sat across from Alice. "I waited until they left. Friends?"

"People from high school."

"Ah." With a sigh, Marilyn popped her napkin open and laid it across her lap.

"Everything okay?"

She met Alice's gaze. "It will be. Jonathan issues."

"Anything I can help with?"

Marilyn looked away and opened her menu. "No, it's related to his job. We can talk later. God, I'm starving. What looks good to you? It's on the campaign tonight, so order what you want. Let's get a bottle of wine, because we may be here for a while."

Great. What she wanted was a long, sultry night in bed with her boss. She'd hoped for an appetizer dinner with a Manhattan and then a romp at some secluded hideaway motel spot inland.

Hell, she'd settle for a go in the backseat of her SUV in a parking lot somewhere. Not happening. Of course.

"I'm sorry Jonathan's having trouble at work."

"Eh." Marilyn shrugged. "It will work itself out. He's been offered a job in Texas."

Her stomach jolted. "What?"

Marilyn shot her a look. "He's not taking it, of course. I put my foot down."

There was a part of her that wanted to react, but emotionally, she couldn't figure out how. If Jonathan got another job out of state, perhaps Marilyn would push him for a divorce sooner, rather than later. Or, if he took the job and they were still married, at least he'd be out of the picture—for themselves and for the campaign.

And perhaps a gradual separation, using the job as an excuse during the campaign, could be a good thing and a natural progression to divorce down the road.

On the other hand, the two of them living in different states might not bode well for Marilyn's political efforts. People will ask questions. The press will *definitely* ask questions.

Perception is everything. Remember?

"Of course."

There was no way Marilyn would make a move toward a divorce until after the election. They'd discussed the timing at length and had agreed—no divorces until well after she'd secured the senate seat. And to her knowledge, Jonathan didn't even know that Marilyn *wanted* a divorce.

Did Jonathan even know that Marilyn was bisexual? Alice didn't think so.

So, there was that additional complication.

Well then, so be it.

Marilyn had her reasons. Alice? Different story.

"I'm getting the crab cakes," Marilyn said.

Alice looked up. "I'm filing for divorce."

MARILYN FOCUSED ON THE MENU. PERHAPS SHE'D GET dessert tonight. Why the hell not? She'd not eaten a bite all day. Nothing but coffee and water and she was famished.

I'm filing for divorce.

Slowly, she lifted her gaze, letting a few seconds slip by so she could fully comprehend, and perhaps contemplate, Alice's words. After a moment, she stared directly at her.

"You're what?"

Alice leaned forward, her voice little more than a whisper. "I'm getting the ball rolling on my divorce. Ella is home for the summer so we can ease her into reality before fall—college for her and, of course, the campaign for us. Life is going to get crazy. Things with Ella—and even with George—are confusing. I need things to move forward."

"Ella is nineteen years old. Almost twenty. She's a grown woman, Alice. She doesn't need your coddling." *But that's what you do.*

Alice's expression didn't break. "It is still difficult for her."

"And that makes you feel guilty."

"Perhaps. Or maybe it's just that I want to get through this with as few challenges as possible. I want a relationship with my daughter that is not strained. It's been that way since Christmas."

Marilyn stared, a jab of anger poking its head up inside her. She knew about the Christmas fiasco, and every time Alice mentioned it since, her anxiety increased. A couple of teenage girls could have destroyed everything they'd worked toward in an instant, spreading rumors all over Tuckaway Bay.

Fortunately, that hadn't happened.

The talk of Alice being gay had not included Marilyn and had not gone beyond Alice's friends—and the walls of the Sea Glass Inn. It hadn't become public knowledge, and that's the way she wanted to keep it. Their standard M.O., of course, was to deny everything, if it came to that—though no one had approached them with any clarification of any supposed rumors.

But if Alice filed for divorce....

"We agreed no movement on this until after the election." Marilyn continued the conversation in a hushed tone. "Well after, I might add. I want to be entrenched in the Senate before we even hint to anyone that we are a couple."

Alice just stared at her, a rather deadpan expression on her face. "I get that," she said. "And I agree it's not the right time for you—but it is for me. I can't go on like this, living with George and pretending we are the happy couple."

Marilyn interrupted. "But we had a plan. We agreed."

Alice inhaled deeply, then sighed. "I understand that, too. But I need to do this now, for my mental health. I need to get things moving...for me. As far as anyone has to know, you are not involved in my life outside of work. So, this isn't about you."

She studied her briefly. "Anything that involves you, involves me."

"Not necessarily. Not to the public."

The look on Alice's face was almost one of defiance—and frankly, unlike her. This was a side of her she'd rarely seen. Oh, they'd argue occasionally, and sometimes Alice would dig in, but Marilyn could sway her over to her viewpoint—even if Alice didn't one hundred percent come on board.

But this? No. She had to convince her not to move yet.

Leaning closer over the table, she whispered. "Alice, you do not want to challenge me on this. Do you understand?"

Five

George heard the front door open and close, then glanced at the clock on his nightstand. Eleven-forty-two. Long damn campaign strategy dinner. He lay there in bed listening, following Alice's trek through the house. She latched the deadbolt, dropped her keys in the glass bowl on the hall table, and then kicked off her heels, probably leaving them by the door.

Her footsteps muffled as she padded down the hall and entered the kitchen. A cabinet door opened and softly closed again. The lights under the cabinets would go on and off with her movement, lighting up the room as needed, so she wouldn't turn on the overhead light.

The refrigerator whined as she drew water from the dispenser. A few silent seconds ticked by as she drank her water, George supposed. Then came the clink of her glass on the stone countertop.

After that, nothing.

Usually, she'd make her way quietly upstairs and into the bedroom across the hall, but tonight, her footsteps were silent. Curious, George got up, pulled on a T-shirt over his boxers, and headed downstairs.

When he got to the kitchen, the motion lights were off, but he could see Alice standing at the sink window, looking out toward the sound. A security light between their house and their neighbor's lit up the backyard and silhouetted her against the night. She stood there still, unmoving, staring pointlessly, it seemed.

She often took to the water when troubled. The sound side of Tuckaway Bay had always been her preference, rather than the ocean side—except for when she'd escape to Quigley Pier. That was her go-to place when she needed to get away from the house and the family.

But more often than not, she'd gravitate to the sound. She'd grown up in this house and called the sound her sanctuary. There were times she'd sit at the end of the dock behind their property late into the night to contemplate things. She found peace there, she'd told him more than once.

What peace did she seek tonight?

He had to wonder.

"Alice?" he whispered.

She didn't immediately respond, but after a few seconds, turned her head slightly his way. "Go back to bed, George. I'm fine."

"Are you?"

The cabinet lights blinked on with her movement. Facing him, he could see her tears.

"Honestly? No, I'm not. George, we have to do something."

"What do you mean?"

She sighed. "I can't live like this any longer."

He took a step closer.

Waving her hands, perhaps signaling him to stop, she said, "Don't come closer. I can't do this if you are standing too close."

"Do what? Alice?"

She sniffled and glanced away for a few seconds, then made eye contact again. "I can't deal with the stress of work, Marilyn's campaign, and our pending divorce. Ella's coming home for the summer has only escalated the tension around here. Don't get me wrong, I love her being home, but the three of us in this house... For my sanity, George, we need to make some decisions."

Panic seized his chest, squeezing the breath out of him. While he knew this was coming, he hadn't expected it tonight. "Decisions."

She nodded. "Yes. We should talk to Ella. We need to separate soon, officially, and file for divorce."

He risked taking another step closer. "But I thought you were waiting until after November? Wasn't that always the plan?"

"Not my plan. That is Marilyn's plan."

No, too soon. I'm not ready. I thought I had more time.

"Maybe you could move to the cabin for the summer. You love the mountains anyway. Then I could spend time with Ella and help her get over this bump in our lives."

"I feel like what's happening with us is more than a bump." How dare she minimize the seriousness of their situation? They were ending their marriage.

"Goodness. You know what I mean. And of course, it is."

"Don't you think helping Ella with this transition is something we should do together?"

"I think conflicting viewpoints will confuse her. Besides, I need to rebuild our relationship. The two of you are tight as a drum."

George cleared his throat. "And I think having one viewpoint in her ear for an entire summer—*yours*—is totally shutting me out of the discussion. No. I'm not moving to the cabin. Besides, I have the play, and it's too far to drive from there every day."

She blinked and appeared to be thinking about that. "I forgot about the play."

"Not surprised," he said. "You're not thinking much about anything Ella and I are doing this summer. You're basically only into yourself, and Alice, that is not like you. Perhaps you need to rethink your priorities."

She stood still, and he watched her eyes close. It felt as if she were shutting him out. Again. Suddenly, the under-cabinet lights went out, thrusting them both into darkness. He blinked rapidly until his eyes adjusted to the dim light in the room. The brief darkness was almost comforting.

Alice waved her arms, and the lights came on again, jerking him back to reality.

"George," she began. "You are right. I need to focus on priorities, and that is precisely why I need some time alone. I can't focus if I can't stop long enough to catch my breath."

"I'm not the one causing your chaos, Alice. My life, Ella's life…we haven't changed. It's your life, your job, your *affair* with Marilyn that is causing the stress."

"No!"

Alice rarely shouted, and it surprised him. Raising her voice was not something she liked to do. He didn't respond.

"No," she said again, this time more quietly. "I need time to think. Granted, Marilyn's run for the Senate is taking its toll, but so is the wishy-washy way we are approaching *our* divorce. We can't decide. We put it off. And I can't do that any longer. Either you or I should leave the house, George. By law, we need to live apart for a year before we can get a divorce. We've already wasted so much time. And since this is my family home, my parents' home, I think you should be the one to leave."

She was right, of course. He wanted no claim to her home. It has always been hers. It was her inheritance. And while he could cite that it was marital property, he wouldn't do that. Besides, he had the cabin in the mountains, his family cabin for generations.

"You know I've made a commitment to the outdoor drama this summer."

"Then maybe get an apartment? A short-term rental?"

He shook his head. "That's money I don't want to spend." That thought reminded him that they also needed to make sure all of their finances were split. They'd already done some things, but not others.

"Well, I don't know what to tell you then, George, but we need to figure this out."

All he could do was stare. Who was this woman standing before him? The one he'd lived with and loved for over two decades? She was stressed, he knew that. Should he just give in and let her have what she wants? At least for now?

To be honest, he hadn't given up hope they would eventually get back together. But if he left…? Then would that hope die?

"Alice…."

"Mom, Dad. Stop."

They both turned. Ella had slipped into the room.

"Honey, go back to bed," Alice said.

"No."

George watched his daughter glance from him to Alice and back again.

"I need to be part of this conversation."

"That will only complicate things." Alice sighed and turned away. "Your father and I will decide."

But Ella wasn't having it, apparently. She faced him fully. "Dad, let's go live at the cabin this summer. You and me. I know you have the play, but possibly you could skip it this year. You have an assistant, right? Maybe you could work one day a week, or two. And maybe this summer you don't want to be tied down to it at all. Let's go, get away, just you and me like we used to do when I was little, and Mom had to work. We could fish, hike, whatever. I would love that."

George studied Ella's expression and realized that if he didn't grab onto this opportunity now, when his daughter was reaching out to him, the time might pass him by. She was a young woman now. How many more years would she want to hike and fish with her old man? Few.

Perhaps with Ella, he'd found the hope he'd thought he'd lost. He might lose his wife, but this beautiful daughter of his? No way. He would never lose her.

"I think that's a wonderful idea. Let's do it."

Ella beamed and jumped closer, hugging him around the neck.

Alice interjected. "I'm not sure that's a good plan."

George broke their embrace and looked at his wife. "To be honest, Alice, I disagree. I think it's an excellent plan."

"And so do I," Ella said.

"It gives you time to think. To figure things out."

Alice's facial expression raced from worried to horrified. "But I wanted to spend the summer with Ella." She looked at their daughter. "Honey, you know since last Christmas things have been strained between us. I wanted some alone time with you. For us to mend some fences."

Ella stared at her for several heartbeats. "Mom, not now. I need time with Dad. Perhaps toward the end of summer, before I go back to school."

Alice grimaced and sighed. "All right. If you are sure."

"I am."

"Then it's settled." George searched his daughter's eyes. "I like this plan. I'll make the arrangements with the production tomorrow, and then you and I can pack up and get out of here."

Ella beamed, and he kissed her forehead.

Turning, George eyed Alice. "And you will get exactly what you wanted—time alone. And I sincerely hope that you take every minute of that time to truly think over what you want for the rest of your life, Alice. Because when I come back late summer, we are moving forward."

Alice said nothing. After a few seconds, she brushed past him and Ella and then headed upstairs.

George had to wonder—did the woman truly know what she wanted?

In her bedroom, Marilyn slipped out of her jacket and draped it over the chair in the corner. Trying to be as quiet as possible, she slipped off her heels and set them aside, then unzipped her skirt and stepped out of it, too. Her fingers roamed over the buttons of her blouse as she unfastened them, easing her arms out of the silky fabric, and then carefully folding and laying it next to the jacket.

The room was dim, lit only by a sliver of light coming from the ensuite bathroom and the half-closed door between the rooms. Jonathan lay snoring in bed, and she didn't want to disturb him. She was not up for another discussion.

Wearing only her panties and a camisole, she eased between the sheets on her side of the bed, careful not to wake him. He had an early morning, and the last thing she wanted was to wake up next to a grouchy husband. She lay on her side facing the light from the bathroom. He lay with his back to her, facing the opposite direction.

They often slept back-to-back. It meant nothing other than that neither enjoyed facing the middle. She was slightly claustrophobic and panicked whenever something covered her face or was too close. He always said he felt safer facing the door, his back to her, protecting her.

She supposed that was all very romantic. He had always sheltered her. And probably that was a very man-thing to do—positioning oneself in such a way to protect the woman.

Whatever. She was simply happy she could sleep and breathe easily, facing the open space.

Involuntarily, she sighed. Deeply. She'd not meant to. Total instinctive reflex.

"Are you having an affair?"

Jonathan's words came from nowhere, seemingly adrift over the bed and into the night, lingering over the space between them. Tempting and teasing. *Confess*, they seemed to say. *It's alright. Go on, you want to get that burden off your chest. Don't you?*

She turned toward the middle of the bed. He didn't.

"What kind of question is that? You know I am not."

He remained silent. The seconds ticked off silently—perhaps measuring the sincerity of her response.

"Jonathan?"

"I think I should take the job in Texas. Honestly, babe, you don't have time for me. These next few months are going to be busier than the past few. I doubt you will miss me, so I should just get out of your way."

Her heart seized a little. His tone was slightly unnerving. He sounded sad and vulnerable. Unlike him. Was taking the job in Texas just a way to get out of her hair? Her life?

"Jonathan," she whispered, laying a hand on his shoulder. "You know I don't want you to go to Texas. I need you here."

"You need me because you don't want a scandal right now."

"What are you talking about...scandal?" She scooted closer. "There are no scandals, honey. No skeletons in my closet, or yours. I need you here because I love you."

He turned fully and met her gaze. She saw the skepticism in his eyes.

"It would be a scandal if we separated. Divorced. It would probably kill your chance at the Senate seat."

"Jonathan, this is ridiculous. We are not separating or getting a divorce. I can't imagine my life without you. Hell, we've been together over thirty years, counting high school. I want you with me."

"Because you love me."

"Yes!"

"You don't need me to lean on? To rub your back and your feet at the end of a long day? To relieve your stress at night? To partner with you on this journey you have chosen?"

Marilyn searched his eyes. "Of course I need you for those things. I admit it. I don't know what I would do without you. You've been my rock for years."

He sat up and stared. "Seriously, Marilyn? What the fuck? Give me a break."

Shit. She had to de-escalate the entire scenario, and fast. "I don't understand why you are mad. What's going on?"

"I already said it. You don't need me. You've already landed me. Conquered me. You have my heart and my soul and my love. I gave all of that to you years ago. But apparently, that isn't enough. You're always seeking the next conquest. First, it was real estate. You ruled that empire and became the top goddamn real estate queen on the East Coast. And now, it's the North Carolina Senate. What's next? Federal government? President?"

"Jonathan...."

"I repeat. You don't need me." He paused, studying her face. "I've spent too many nights, too many weekends, alone. I've done a lot of thinking during that time. And I'll ask again—are you having an affair?"

"No. Of course not. When the fuck would I have time for that?"

"You said that when we lived in Charlotte, too, and you were lying."

She drew in her lower lip, biting it while she peered into his eyes. "Jonathan, I made a huge mistake back then. That was nearly twenty years ago. When I made that promise to you—that I would never be with another man again—I meant it. There is no other man in my life."

He grasped her hand. "You are gone so damn much. I had to ask."

"I'm working, sweetheart."

"I want to believe that, but the old feelings... They crop up. Nag at me."

She edged closer and whispered. "God, you are so wrong, baby. I love you more than you know. And I need you by my side."

"In your campaign, you mean."

"Yes, of course. I need you right beside me during the campaign. We're a team, right? But I need you for even more."

"Really." He lifted his chin. "Then show me. We've not made love in weeks."

Marilyn pulled the camisole over her head and crowded her breasts up against his hot chest. She grasped his hand and pushed it down the front of her panties. He grabbed her there, and she groaned.

"God. I need you, Jonathan. I need *you* and don't you ever forget it. And don't you dare go to fucking Texas and abandon me."

Six

The next morning, Alice watched from the front porch as George and Ella packed up the back end of his SUV. The two were excited, laughing, as Ella shoved things in willy-nilly and George took them out to neatly repack. But that was George—he always went about things in a thoughtful, organized, and methodical way.

I'll miss that about him.

The entire scenario reminded Alice of years past, that same scene playing out with Ella as a much younger child, laughing and eager to get to the mountains. Except in the past, she was in the picture, too.

George closed the SUV and rounded the car to the driver's side with a wave. Ella turned at the passenger door, blew her a kiss, and said, "See you in a few weeks!"

Her girl was excited, and Alice couldn't blame her. Perhaps this was the right thing, after all.

While she'll miss having the summer with Ella, she needed time alone to figure out her next steps—and maybe even how to cope when she missed the things George used to do. How things were when it was the three of them.

But what would she gain?

Her freedom?

The independence to live her own authentic life?

George was wrong, though, about one thing. She didn't need to think about *what she wanted*—she already knew that.

She wanted Marilyn.

No, more than that.

She wanted *a life with Marilyn*, the one she'd craved for so long.

And if she could still have a strong mother-daughter relationship with Ella, and a close friendship with George, she would love that as well.

But her heart craved a life to live together freely, with Marilyn, in their own home, as a couple. Out in the open, with friends and family accepting their choice. No more running around, hiding their affections, sneaking out for clandestine hookups whenever they could manage them.

While those times were often fun and exciting, after more than a dozen years, she was growing weary of the secrecy. And sometimes, she was tired of Marilyn calling all the shots—although she'd never admit that to anyone. Or say that to her. But frankly, she needed to think about that, too.

So, she knew the *what*. The *when* part worried her.

Honestly, there were days she wondered if a life with Marilyn would ever happen. *Are we on the same page?*

Alice scrolled through her phone contacts and located Matt Miller's information. She'd considered email but decided a call was better. She wanted to thank him for his help at last Monday's town hall—and offer him a job. But it all had to happen quickly, and she didn't want to leave it to chance that he'd read his emails today.

She rose and poked her head into Marilyn's office, waiting while she finished a call.

Marilyn glanced up. "Alice?"

"Hey." She moved inside and glanced behind her. No one had slipped into her outer office while she was waiting. "I'm going to step out for a call. Thought I'd pick up coffee. You ready for another one?"

Marilyn picked up her empty to-go cup and shook it. "Yes, please. You know what I like."

"Of course. Give me fifteen minutes. Oh, and remember I'm taking the afternoon off. Let me know if you need a reminder why."

Marilyn grinned. "I remember."

"Great. Back in a few."

She took the stairs down one flight to the ground level, then out to the sidewalk. The coffee shop—Griff's Grinds—sat two blocks down the street. The breeze was warm and salty, the ocean just a couple of blocks over. Even though it was barely nine o'clock in the morning, she could tell the afternoon would be a hot one.

She and Marilyn had not discussed the previous night's dinner. Alice was relieved, although it would have been unusual for Marilyn to bring up their personal life at the office. The subject would come up soon, she was certain. But with George and Ella leaving earlier, plus all the campaign details on her mind, she wasn't in the mood to talk about it, even though she knew that discussion would happen in private, not at the office.

Alice knew Marilyn's office rules very well, and she was not about to break them.

On the way to Griff's, she pulled out her cell phone and dialed Matt. He answered on the second ring.

"Hello?"

"Matt? Hi. It's Alice McBain from the Morgan campaign."

"Hey, Alice. Good to hear from you. Marilyn still flying high?"

"We both are."

"You should be. You pulled off that town hall like nobody's business."

Alice smiled. "Well, your help was greatly appreciated. We needed your insight and support, and we both thank you for your efforts."

"I was happy to do it."

"Good." She paused for a moment, heading into the coffee shop. Griff, the owner, gave her a nod as she entered. He put two fingers up, as if in question, and Alice nodded back. He knew what she wanted.

"Matt, I want to pitch an idea to you and am wondering if you have time later this afternoon, say, around one or two?"

He didn't hesitate. "I'm intrigued, and I do."

"Great. I'll text the address and time. We'll meet downtown."

"I'll be there."

"Super."

She hung up and looked at Griff.

He slid two cups of coffee toward her on the counter. "One large black. One large cold mocha with an espresso shot and extra whip."

The mocha, of course, was hers. "Perfect." She handed over a twenty and waved off the change.

He promptly deposited the remainder in the tip jar. "How's the campaign going?"

"About to heat up," Alice responded. "I may need to start a coffee tab."

Griff laughed. "Anytime. Coffee fuels the world, you know." He pointed to a sign over his head that said just that.

Alice laughed. She liked Griff. She'd joked with Marilyn once that Griff was an edgier George. He was older than her, probably in his fifties, and very kind to every soul who walked into his coffee shop. Like George, he was thoughtful and caring, running his little business like a well-tuned machine. What gave him the edge was his rather Bohemian lifestyle—living in the studio apartment above the coffee shop—his shaggy gray hair and beard, and his collection of Grateful Dead T-shirts, which were, apparently, his uniform.

Not to mention the steady flow of Dead music rolling through the coffee shop.

She tipped her mocha and smiled. "Um. Good. Later, Griff."

"Have a great day, Alice."

I intend to! She headed back to the office, resolved that she needed an attitude shift. No matter how busy she was, or what was going on in her life, it didn't hurt—and probably helped—to remain positive.

Now I'm sounding like Lia.

At the thought of her friend, she wondered how things were going at Sea Glass Inn, over on the ocean side of Tuckaway Bay. Lia, one of her college besties, ran the resort beach hotel with her husband,

Zach. Their friend, Maggie, was also there for the summer, staying at The Gull Cottage with her kids. And Julia, another college roommate, lived just a few miles down the sound side of the coast with her significant other, Sam.

She needed a girlfriend lunch. These women were her people, and she didn't like letting time go by without seeing them.

It had been a while. They'd not been together since Carol Oliver's high school graduation in late May.

Quickly, she voicemailed herself a memo: *Arrange lunch with the girls.*

She scurried on toward the town hall and her office. There were several things to get off her plate that morning before taking the afternoon off. When she got there, she realized she'd missed Marilyn, who had been railroaded into an impromptu meeting with David Callahan. She'd jotted a note and left it on Alice's desk: *In meeting with D.C. Bring coffee.*

She did as Marilyn asked, quietly interrupting the meeting in David's office. The expression on Marilyn's face was puzzling, and Alice knew one thing for certain—Marilyn wanted to be anywhere but there.

She thanked Alice for the coffee and dismissed her, turning to David.

Alice slipped out the door and carried on with her morning.

At fifteen minutes to one, Marilyn was still meeting with David. Alice sent her a text saying she was leaving and then walked the three blocks to the town park. Tuckaway Bay had recently renovated its small-town square, adding a gazebo smack in the center. She'd asked Matt to meet her there earlier when she'd texted him.

They arrived at the same time.

Matt held out his hand, and Alice shook it. "So glad you could make it, Matt."

"My pleasure."

"Let's sit a minute." She motioned to the bench seats inside the gazebo. "This turned out nice, didn't it?"

"Very." He glanced about. "Wasn't this one of Marilyn's projects?"

Alice nodded. "It was. The old amphitheater that used to be here was unsafe and an eyesore. Marilyn sought grant opportunities to get it cleaned up."

"I thought so." Again, Matt looked around. "Was David Callahan in on that project?"

Alice shook her head. "No. That was before he came. Why do you ask?" She found it very interesting that he would bring up David. And maybe it made her a little suspicious.

"No reason other than I know he's a grant writer."

She debated whether she should say the words on her mind, then put them out there. Matt's reaction might tell her a few things. "He *did* work on grants for the town."

Matt met her gaze. "Did? That sounds like past tense."

Alice blew out a breath. "Yeah, well... This is not common knowledge, but it will be soon. David resigned yesterday. Gave his two weeks' notice."

"Hm. Interesting." He cocked his head, studying Alice. "I'm surprised at that."

"Why?"

Glancing away momentarily, he shrugged. "I don't really know him. In fact, I met him for the first time the other night at the town hall. We chatted casually—but he seemed very interested in Marilyn and the campaign. He asked a lot of questions. When he learned I was a volunteer, he inquired how he could volunteer, too."

"For Marilyn?"

He nodded. "Why, yes. Of course."

"Interesting...."

"Why so?"

Alice let a few seconds tick by. "Because he's going to work for Fred Faust as his campaign communications manager."

Matt stared. "Seriously?"

"As a heart attack."

"Wow."

"Right?" Alice shifted in her seat, glanced across the street, and then stood. Time to get on with it. "Matt, I have a proposition for you."

"Oh?"

She faced him. "I know you're starting grad school in the fall, so if this interferes, just say so. Come join the team and help us get Marilyn into the Senate."

He stood. "I'm in."

"But you haven't heard what I want you to do."

He waved her off. "It doesn't matter. I'll put graduate school off until the spring semester. I'll do whatever you want me to do for two reasons. I want the experience of working in politics, for one, but even more, I want Marilyn to win."

"Tell me why." Alice squared herself and met his gaze head-on. She wanted to look him in the eye when he responded.

He didn't mince words. "Alice, I'm a gay Black man living and working in a white straight man's world—and in the South. I'm liberal. I like her agenda. I want change. And I think Marilyn can do that."

Alice grinned. In fact, her lips hurt from how wide her grin went.

It was true Marilyn was fighting an uphill battle. LGBTQ+ rights, abortion rights, First Amendment rights, and more were her priorities. No one predicted she could win the state—North Carolina was still very conservative, even if pockets of progressive thinking existed —but Marilyn was not one to back down. While the North Carolina Senate held a Republican conservative majority, the past several governors were Democrats.

There was hope.

She pointed across the street. "You see that building for rent over there? In about thirty minutes, you and I will walk over there and meet the owner. We're going to see if it meets our needs for the campaign headquarters. And if it does, we will sign a six-month lease. And then after that, it will be your responsibility to get the campaign up and running in full force, under my direction. I want volunteers. I want a field campaign. I want media attention. I want a schedule of events and town halls across the state. And I want donors."

He smiled. "Anything else?"

"I guess I should also say that I want you to be my assistant campaign manager."

"Consider it done."

Alice breathed a sigh of relief. She reached out and shook his hand. "We didn't discuss salary."

Matt laughed. "It doesn't matter. I'm just out of college. I'm used to living on ramen. Besides, I'm living with my parents for the summer, and my mom will be thrilled for me to extend that into the fall. Anything that works for your budget is fine with me."

Nothing could have pleased her more. "Marilyn is going to be elated. Thanks, Matt." She glanced at the clock in the town center. "Now, let's go look at that space."

Seven

When Alice entered Marilyn's office two hours later, she immediately noticed the stressed, concerned, but also questioning look on her boss's face. *How long had the meeting with Callahan gone?* She was more than curious about the subject of that meeting.

"Well?" Marilyn asked.

Alice sat in the leather chair opposite her. "We scored big today."

Marilyn's grin widened. "Matt?"

"He's all in."

"Excellent."

Alice bent closer and lowered her voice. "And the space down the street is perfect."

"More good news." Marilyn leaned back in her chair, glanced at her calendar, and tossed a pen aside. "I need a break. Had lunch yet?"

"No."

"Let's grab a quick bite across the street at the Grill. I have a four o'clock, so that gives us nearly an hour."

Excited to share with Marilyn all that had transpired earlier, she agreed. "I'm famished. Lead the way."

They left their offices, closing the outer door and leaving a note on a whiteboard saying they would return by three-forty-five.

The Salt Beach Grill was hopping for mid-afternoon on a Thursday—but Alice knew that was exactly the reason Marilyn chose it for their late lunch. The crowd was loud, animated, and high energy —the place filled with locals and tourists alike. Summer was in full force across the island.

Alice knew they could talk freely there. No one would overhear.

Also, the more people around meant she might do a little informal campaigning—if the opportunity arose. People were recognizing her potential beyond the mayor of Tuckaway Bay in this small town. Plus, tourists.

"Two?" The host put up two fingers. "Right this way."

They followed her to a corner high-top table looking out over the town square. She and Marilyn found their seats and opened the menus placed there by the host.

"Sierra will be over to get your drinks in a few."

"Great." Alice smiled. "Thanks."

Marilyn sighed, set her menu aside, and made direct eye contact. "I know what I want. Tell me about Matt. Is he excited?"

"Super excited. We should talk budget soon. He's not expecting much, but we should pay him what he's worth. We have the funds."

"Is he willing to fundraise?"

"He'll do whatever it takes. Whatever we ask."

Marilyn chewed on her lip, glancing out the window. "I know he's worth a lot, but let's start him low with incentives for more. How did you pitch his responsibilities?"

"Assistant campaign manager, answering to me. He'd run the headquarters, seek volunteers, schedule events, manage a field campaign, donors, and media. I know that's a heavy workload—but I'll be doing some of that, too."

"He could delegate some of the minor tasks to volunteers and oversee the rest."

"Yes, exactly my thoughts."

"And the more money he brings in, we incrementally increase his salary."

Alice nodded. "Also, my thoughts. Or provide bonuses. I'll have to look into the restrictions on that."

"You will still manage the budget, direct contacts with the big donors, confirm venues, review contracts, and the like. I still want you as my right-hand woman, Alice. Plus, you are my strategic partner."

She reached under the table for Alice's hand and wove their fingers together. Alice squeezed back.

"Your strategic partner and more," she whispered.

Marilyn smiled. "About last night...."

Alice broke their grasp and brought her hands up to the table. "No. We will not get into that today."

"We're not?" Marilyn looked a little shocked.

She leaned closer. "Look. I realize I've been on edge, but I'm turning a new leaf. Hiring Matt will help. You should also know that George and Ella left for the mountains this morning. They plan to be gone most of the summer."

Marilyn looked puzzled. "But what about the play? Doesn't George have that?"

"I think he worked something out. The thing is... This gives me time to get my house in order. To chill out a minute and decide on the next steps."

"*Your* next steps."

"Yes. Of course. I'm not putting any timeline on you."

Marilyn stared, her eyes flicking back and forth. "What are you thinking? And when?"

Taking a risk, Alice grasped Marilyn's hand on top of the table. They were friends, right? No one would think anything of it. "About the when. I know the timing is not right for you. I know we have to wait, sweetheart. But when the time is right for me, I want to be ready. Mentally, emotionally, and...financially. When it's time, I won't want to wait—I want nothing in our way. Especially if it involves my family. I want them comfortable with the future, not fighting me on this. It feels like we've waited a lifetime, and I just—"

"Shh..." Marilyn interrupted, pulling away her hand. "Shush, my darling," she whispered. "When the time comes, we will both know. And we both will be ready."

Under the table, Marilyn kicked off her heels and ran her bare toes up one side of Alice's calf. That simple action sent a shiver through her that felt like the early days of their relationship.

BAYSIDE REALTY, YEARS EARLIER

ALICE ROSE FROM HER DESK AND BLINKED. SHE'D STARED too long at the listing copy and contracts. Her nagging headache had not subsided—but she needed to tidy up the offices. Fishing her dust cloth from the desk drawer, she rose and glanced around the lobby.

Time to get to this last task.

Looking past her L and out the front window, she knew it was well after five-thirty. Dusk had settled over the island town, and a steady beam of traffic lights rolled by on the main street. She should get home soon. Ella had homework, she was certain, and George most likely had dinner nearly on the table. She was fortunate to have a man who cooked. Honestly, the guy doted on her to excess, and she suddenly felt so grateful.

Her temple still throbbing, she glanced at her coffee cup. It had been a while since she'd had any caffeine. Perhaps that, and an aspirin, would help.

Tossing the cloth aside, she grabbed her mug and started for the kitchenette, noticing a light on in an office down the hall. She'd been so engrossed in her work the past few hours she'd barely spoken to a soul—and honestly wasn't certain who had left for the day.

But that light—that office. Alice knew exactly who was still there.

With a sigh, she moved on into the kitchenette.

A half-pot of cold coffee sat on the Bunn coffeemaker. *Great.* She could have predicted that no one would have cleaned it up. *Good old Alice. She'll take care of it.* Heaven help the agent who accepted the fate of coffee duty or took the initiative to make a new pot.

Clean or no caffeine.

She should make a sign. Chuckling to herself, she poured a cold cup, added a little blue packet of sweetener, and slid it into the microwave to reheat.

While waiting, she swiped a damp dishcloth over the coffeemaker and cleaned up some spills and grounds on the counter. After a moment, she tossed the rag aside and stared at the countdown of numbers on the microwave while absentmindedly massaging the back of her neck. It was a poor attempt to ease away some of the tension that had settled there.

"Here. Let me."

The voice came from behind. Alice didn't have to turn around to know it was Marilyn. Her back twitched a little. Had she intentionally snuck up on her?

"What?" She semi-turned.

Marilyn slowly brushed Alice's hair to the side, smoothing her palm over one shoulder. Her cool fingertips wandered and began a slow knead at the base of Alice's neck. A sizzle of something foreign raced down Alice's back, and she sharply, involuntarily, exhaled. Marilyn's touch did nothing to ease her brick-tight muscles. She only tensed more.

"Relax, Alice," she whispered. "I'm not going to bite."

Oh, please don't go there. "I know that."

Still, she responded with a slight jerk.

Why the hell is my body reacting like this? I've never before had a physical, sexual response to a woman.

Marilyn angled herself closer, laying a hand on her other shoulder. "You didn't come out of your little space all day," she whispered. "You should come out once in a while. All work and no play makes Alice a dull girl, or so they say... You know?"

She turned and caught Marilyn's eye. *She thinks I'm dull.* "I came out for coffee and to pee. Twice."

Marilyn laughed.

And even though Alice looked straight ahead, staring at the cabinets, she imagined Marilyn's head tossed back with her long dirty-blond mane billowing down her back, her face lit up with pleasure.

She relaxed. A bit.

Marilyn's hands slipped from her neck to her shoulders and

massaged her flesh and muscle. "God, you're tight. I'm going to make a rule for you."

"Oh?" Alice was intrigued. What did she mean?

"Yes. You can no longer sit for more than an hour at that desk without getting up."

"And where should I go?"

Marilyn leaned closer and said softly. "You can always come visit me, Alice. I'd like that." She pressed hard into Alice's shoulders, the pressure bordered on pain...and felt so good.

Alice released a deep sigh.

"There," Marilyn murmured. "That's it, sweetie. Let it go."

Despite her helpful, make-everyone-happy personality, Alice wasn't a touchy-feely woman. She was a bit like her friend Julia, in that way. She didn't roll into a crowd giving hugs and didn't particularly want them in return. In fact, she didn't like most people touching her at all—but for some odd reason, Marilyn's hands on her body were welcome. She didn't mind her fingers running over her neck, shoulders...skin. No, not one bit.

Submit.

Her shoulder muscles relaxed. "Oh... Yes," she whispered. *I didn't know I was so tense. How good it felt to let go.*

"Finally," Marilyn purred, her lips dangerously close to Alice's ear. "Your shoulders are hard as steel. Goodness, Alice, you need some serious downtime."

I need something.

"We're going to remedy that. Dinner?"

"Tonight?"

"Of course."

Alice quickly turned, facing Marilyn, her back jammed up against the counter. It was like she'd suddenly awoken from a hazy dream. One she couldn't quite remember but was vividly embedded, deeply lodged, somewhere in her being.

She blinked again, repeatedly, and pushed past Marilyn. "Thanks, but no. My family, *my husband*... Is waiting for me. I have to get home."

Alice rushed out of the kitchenette. The dusting could wait until morning.

"YOU KNOW, THESE FISH TACOS ARE SUPERB. I COULD EAT them every day."

At the Salt Beach Grill, Alice watched Marilyn as she enjoyed the last bite of her lunch and then took a drink of ice water.

"My crab cakes were good, too. Exceptional, actually."

Marilyn nodded. "I heard they have a new chef in the back. Good move, I'd say." She set her plate to the side and reached into her bag for her cell phone.

Alice waited while she checked her messages and responded to a couple of texts or emails. Their lunch finished, they'd lingered longer than either of them had intended, but she was happy for the alone time, even amid the summer chaos.

Marilyn placed the phone face down on the table and looked up. "I moved my four o'clock to tomorrow morning. No need to rush out of here yet."

Alice felt a grin spread across her face. "Good. That gives us some time to chat."

"Yes. We need to strategize more about Matt's role and discuss a few other things."

She wondered if they were on the same page. "Right. So, tell me. What's going on with Callahan? You two were huddled up in there for hours."

Marilyn exhaled and relaxed against the back of her chair.

Alice immediately knew she was worried.

"It was rather strange, to be honest," she began. "He called the meeting because he wanted to discuss his last two weeks and his transition out—but it quickly morphed into something I hadn't expected —and I'm not sure I handled it well, to be honest."

That piqued her interest. "How so?"

Marilyn leaned closer and lowered her voice. "He was pushing hard for me to support Gale Barker as the interim city manager. He has this whole damn plan worked out—how he would train Gale during the transition, getting him up to speed, and all that. How Gale would train someone from his office, and so on, to replace him. Which is all fine and the way it's normally done. But... Apparently, he and Gale have already met with the council and laid out their plan."

That totally seemed out of line. "*Their plan?* With no one else's input? What the hell? Did he show you this plan?"

Marilyn's eyes grew wider. "Oh yes. I asked for a copy, but he only had one hard copy with him and was very stingy about what I could see—you know, covering parts up with his forearm and not flipping through all the pages. I told him to email it to me, which is why I checked my phone a few minutes ago. He hasn't yet, so I just now emailed him again."

Curious. "What is the plan?"

"It's ridiculous, is what it is. He wants to change the org structure."

"Excuse me? He's on his way out. Why would he care?"

"Exactly. And supposedly, according to him, the city council loves it."

"Did you know he met with the council?" It seemed odd that Marilyn, the Mayor, wouldn't know about a council meeting. But the council was basically David's employer, so....

"No, I didn't. I suppose he didn't have to tell me, but for good relationships inside the city government, it would have been nice. Especially since Gale and I will work closely together after David leaves."

Alice sat back, thinking. "This makes little sense. I can see him recommending someone for the interim position, but protocol says you don't make those kinds of decisions on your own. You get input, and there is a procedure, I'm sure. But Gale Barker? Why him? He's over planning and zoning. Did David make a case for him, qualifications and all? And who would replace Gale?"

"Oh sure. He has it all worked out. I don't get it, but evidently the council did."

"Tell me about this org structure."

Marilyn took a breath, paused before letting it out slowly, and searched Alice's eyes. "The structure cut some positions, added others."

"Such as?"

Again, she waited. "Since Tuckaway Bay is growing, he says, the town needs a deputy mayor. So, he added that position to the organizational chart. He wants to enlarge the zoning and planning division, which I actually agree with given the growth of the community and my experience in real estate. He wants to combine the city clerk and finance departments into one division. Not ideal, but perhaps doable. The dangerous change he wants to make is to merge the fire department, EMS, and beach rescue into one division—but he also wants to cut staff, stating the town has adequate rescue services via the coast guard. I have serious safety concerns about that."

"But why? The beach is a tourist draw. A destination. And it needs to be safe. I don't understand why he would eliminate staff and services."

"Looks to me like he's cutting administrative costs across the divisions so there is money for the deputy mayor."

"I don't get why the town needs that."

Marilyn stared off for a few seconds. "I hate to say it, but if his scenario plays out, then the mayor, deputy mayor, and city manager would all work together, and you know how that can go with a threesome."

Alice stared back blankly.

"Someone always gets left out—or at least doesn't get the attention they want."

Got it. I think. "So, David leaves and works for Faust. Gale takes his place as city manager. The council appoints a deputy. That's four people, not a threesome. Right? You, me, Gale, and whoever."

"Not exactly."

"Why?"

"Alice, sweetheart, he wants to eliminate your position."

For as long as Alice could remember, there had always been an assistant to the mayor position in their local government. In fact, she personally knew the three people who held the position before she took over. "I don't get it."

"I know. They—he and Gale—claim it's an unnecessary position with the addition of the deputy."

Alice sat looking at Marilyn, feeling a little dumbfounded. "Well, that's stupid. I do a ton of menial tasks, like running copies or fetching coffee or scheduling meetings—not that those things are not important, because they are. I take pride in doing those behind-the-scenes tasks because I know those are the tasks that make the machine run smoother. They think a deputy mayor wants to stand at the copy machine all afternoon?"

Marilyn touched her hand. "I know. It's ridiculous. You really keep things moving, and your job is so necessary—but I could not convince him of that."

"They want me out of the picture for a reason."

She nodded. "It's because of what I said, a threesome. They don't want you and me to side together and be a cog in whatever wheel they are building. They have something up their sleeves, and I just can't figure out what it is."

Alice sighed. "When will this go into effect?"

Marilyn squeezed her hand. "Remember, it's all tentative at this point. But David has a few more days to convince the council that this is the way to go. Of course, I will voice my concerns. But honestly, Alice? It might happen soon."

"So, I'm out of a job?" She stared past Marilyn toward the park. "I just don't understand it. All this is whirling around in my brain. Why does David even care? He's leaving?" *And maybe even a better question.* "Why all this change now?"

Marilyn leaned closer, whispering. "I don't know. Let's think about all of this. We need a plan."

"Of course." Then she remembered her earlier conversation with Matt. "You know, Matt said something interesting today."

"About the campaign?"

"No." She hesitated. "About David. Not sure if it's anything, but he said David asked him about volunteering for your campaign the other night at the town hall."

"David? Volunteering for us? That makes no sense. He's going to work for Faust."

"I know. But then why the hell was he asking Matt about volunteering for you?"

"I don't know, but I guarantee you Fred Faust is involved." Marilyn's face turned a little pale. "David is speaking out of both sides of his mouth and playing politics whether or not he wants to admit it. I don't trust him, or Gale Barker, and frankly, most of the city council."

"What do we do now?"

"Keep our eyes and ears open—and watch our damn backs."

Eight

Two days later, the Tuckaway Bay girls met at the Sea Glass Inn for lunch.

"Alice, I'm so glad you called. We *all* needed this." Lia smiled and reached for her friend's hand. "I'm so grateful to have all of you close by this summer."

The four best friends—Lia, Maggie, Julia, and Alice—clasped hands and squeezed as they waited to order lunch at The Sandcastle Restaurant, on the ground floor of the inn. Menus and water glasses delivered, the ladies chatted casually, the Atlantic rolling toward the surf in the background.

"The beach and the pool are busy today," Alice noted, looking out their ocean view window. Both areas bustled with vacationers. "I'm just glad you could get away for a while, Lia," Alice said. "It's summer, so I know you are busy. I was afraid you'd have to cancel on us."

Lia waved her off. "Oh no. Zach and Belle have everything covered. Zach is still over the restaurant, of course, but he has an assistant now who takes care of all maintenance issues. Belle and I take turns going to lunch, so the office is always covered. She's there now, so I'm good."

"Speaking of Belle," Julia said. "I saw her and baby Grace at Food

Lion yesterday. That child has grown so much. Her chubby little cheeks..." Julia made squeaky baby-talk noises and pretended she was pinching invisible baby cheeks. "I just want to squeeze her."

Alice smiled to herself. Julia sounded good, joyful, and that made her happy. She'd had enough heartache in her life.

"She's almost six months old!" Lia beamed like the grandmother she was. "I can't get enough of her snuggles. Seriously, what did we do before she came? I can't remember life without her."

"Belle seems happy."

Lia's smile narrowed a little. "I think she's content. Gracie was an interruption to her life plans, but a pleasant one. She loves her to pieces."

"Despite all the Christmas chaos, you mean..." Maggie interjected. "That was quite the holiday, wasn't it?"

"Well yes. Truth." Lia tipped her water glass toward her friends.

They all nodded.

"I'll second that," Alice said. They'd all had their share of life's interruptions, herself included.

Julia looked thoughtful, then faced Lia. "You know, I may be crossing into territory you do not want to go into, Lia, so say so if that's true... But I'm curious—has Belle ever found Gracie's father?"

Alice watched Lia's facial expression fall from joy to concern. She shook her head. "No. I think I may have mentioned this back when Belle was pregnant, but it was a one-night thing, here at the hotel, with a guest. She was embarrassed about that, of course, so she didn't tell us for quite a while that she was pregnant."

Maggie leaned in. "But she looked for him, didn't she?"

Lia's chin dropped slightly. "She did. He had disappeared the next morning, and his sister and brother-in-law, who were the registered guests, were also gone. She tried contacting the sister after she found out about the pregnancy to see how to reach him, but there was no answer and a full voicemail box, so she couldn't leave a message. I believe she tried several times. She got no response from email either."

Julia studied Lia. "And he never called?"

"No. And he told her he would." Lia glanced about. "What is it the kids say? He ghosted her, I guess."

"Sounds like it." Julia slowly nodded. "Well, Lia, if he should poke his head up into Belle's world, be sure and let me know. I've dealt with a lot of cases when a missing parent suddenly appears and wants to be a part of the child's life."

Alice registered the shocked look on Lia's face. "Oh, he wouldn't. Would he? Could he...take Gracie?"

"He could ask for joint custody, or visitation rights. So, you need me to make sure everything is handled fairly, and legally."

Lia nodded. "I'll talk to Belle."

"Don't overly concern her, just have her be aware."

"Right."

The conversation lulled momentarily, and Alice felt the need to change the subject. Lia didn't look like she wanted to talk much more about the possibilities. She looked over at Maggie. "You've been quiet the past couple of weeks. How are you holding up? How's life at Gull Cottage?"

Maggie shrugged. "I'm just decompressing after all the family upheaval since Christmas. The kids love it here, of course. Who wouldn't want a summer living right on the beach? Thanks to Lia and Zach." She grinned at Lia. "Carol is working at the inn, as you know, and Jason and Chloe are being lazy bums for the summer."

"And you?"

Maggie grinned. "Oh, I'm good. Now that... Well. Now that the ordeal with Max is over, I've been trying to focus on my family, and myself. I've been painting, which has been total therapy. That, and the sun and sand and surf, of course."

"Give yourself time, Maggie," Lia said.

Julia nodded. "Yes. Beach therapy. It's good for what ails us."

"I believe that."

Alice hesitated. The four of them had not discussed Maggie's estranged husband's death recently, and it appeared she didn't want to talk about it either. "But it's all still fresh, isn't it? What's it been? Three weeks since Max died?"

"And a week since the funeral. I still have his estate to tie up."

"I see." Then, Alice jumped into the *elephant-in-the-room* conversation. "When do you go to Australia? You are still going, right? I hate to think of you going alone."

"I'm not, actually. Carol is going with me."

Julia leaned forward. "Maggie, do you think that is wise?"

"I do. We both need closure."

Lia cocked her head. "But what about this Lilly person? What if you run into her?"

Alice wondered how Maggie would respond to seeing her estranged, and now deceased, husband's baby mama.

But Maggie flashed a sassy smile. "Actually, I hope we do." She paused, glancing at the group. "But enough of that. I want to hear all about the campaign." She swiveled directly toward Alice. "How is *that* going? That Fred Faust character scares me."

"I know," Lia said. "It's like he came out of the woodwork, or woodpile. Something. I didn't even know he existed until the primary commercials started popping up."

"He's disgusting." Julia popped open her menu and started reading.

Alice had hoped to avoid any discussion about the campaign, which is perhaps why she brought up Max, hoping that would delay things a bit—because frankly, she didn't know what to say. What was *safe* for her to share.

She definitely didn't want to talk about the Callahan issue, and the shake-up going on in their local government, and that Alice might lose her job, because she and Marilyn hadn't quite figured out what he was up to. Or how to address it.

She stayed in the safe zone. "We hired an assistant campaign manager this week. Someone to work with me. And we leased an office downtown."

"Wow." Lia's eyes grew round. "That sounds like progress. Are the polls good?"

"Eh. So far, seems she and Faust are running neck-and-neck."

"Ugh," Julia lamented, still perusing her menu. "I'm glad you got some help though."

"Yes. Definitely." Except, now that she'd said the words out loud, she wondered if she'd jinxed herself. If she lost her job with the city, she'd likely be spending more time on the campaign, but could the campaign support a manager and an assistant?

"That should take the pressure off you somewhat?"

She nodded. "It should. I'll have to train him and oversee everything, but having someone on board who can be the legs of the work will definitely help."

"Who did you hire? Anyone we know?" Maggie picked at her napkin.

"Probably not, although he is local. Recent Duke grad. His name's Matt Miller. Loves politics. He's a LGBTQ+ rights advocate, and an enthusiastic Marilyn supporter."

"Well, good. That can't hurt." Julia paused. "I saw Faust on the news this morning. His platform is...well, chilling."

"I know!" Lia jerked her shoulders back. "His stance on women's rights—limiting work hours for pregnant women and those with kids under three but not providing any sort of compensation for their lost work hours. Plus, he's backing reduced S.N.A.P. benefits. That's horrible."

"And don't get me started on the abortion rights issue," Julia added. "Making it illegal to treat a woman who has just had an abortion and needs health care, jailing her and the physician, and then forcing her to get her tubes tied." She took a drink of her ice water and glanced away, disgusted. "Can you believe anyone would even suggest such an archaic thing?"

"That's unethical." Maggie leaned toward Julia. "Are you okay?"

Julia jerked back. "Yes, but he's treating women like criminals! I guarantee you he wouldn't like it if he were forced to have a vasectomy or have his dick removed." She jerked toward Alice. "Would Marilyn support that?"

"Having his dick removed?" Alice stared with wide eyes. "Probably."

They all laughed, then Julia added. "Seriously though, Alice, will she push him on women's reproductive issues?"

Alice slowly nodded. "Marilyn's approach is straightforward. She will lay it all out and state why it's important and focus on the consequences for everyone if rights are violated. But women's issues aren't the only thing on her platform."

"Of course," Maggie said. "She talked about immigration at the town hall. I watched the replay on the local cable news. Plus, she's focused on the democracy versus autocracy issue and transgender rights. I'm sure there is more."

Alice agreed. "Yes, she supports all that. Her platform will become clearer as the summer rolls on. But she won't play hardball—until it's time."

Julia gave Alice a stern look. "She has to play hardball, Alice. Convince her of that. Faust is slimy and will cut her off at the knees— and then jerk out her ovaries."

"Oh, she will. Like I said—when it's time. Marilyn won't come off as the aggressive, in-your-face, trailer-park bitch. She'd be an easy target like that for Faust. She'll play her own game. Just wait and see."

Maggie smacked her hand on the table. "Marilyn is tough. There was a fire in her eyes when she gave that speech. I could see it through the camera lens. She's feisty, and I like that. I have a feeling that if Faust attempts to cut her off at the knees, then she will... Well, she'll cut his dick off."

Lia giggled.

What Maggie said was true. Marilyn was feisty and assertive. She would professionally and persistently stand her ground, not flinching, and never backing down. Alice knew that side of her all too well.

"I guess we'll find out how well she can handle Faust in September," she said. "Earlier this morning, we signed an agreement for a debate in Raleigh."

"Excellent." Julia smiled and leaned back. "I can't wait to see her take him on. Can you get us seats in the room?"

Alice tipped her head and grinned back. "Maybe. I have some insider privileges."

BUT WHEN SHE GOT BACK TO THE OFFICE THAT afternoon, she realized insider privileges would likely get her nowhere

—at least within the current situation at the Tuckaway Bay city government.

Alice stared at her laptop and reread the email. Literally, she was stunned.

Marilyn was going to shit.

The door between their two offices flew open and banged against the wall. Jerking toward the sound, Alice caught the fury in Marilyn's eyes.

"Did you see it?" she shouted.

"I did."

"Get in here." Marilyn turned and went back into her office.

After a moment, which included a deep inhale and a long, cleansing exhale, Alice got up, grabbed a notepad and pen, and joined her, closing the door more quietly than Marilyn had opened it.

Ten days had passed since David Callahan resigned. He officially had four more days of work before leaving. They couldn't pass soon enough.

Nine days earlier, he'd shared his ideas with Marilyn for restructuring several city departments and a new staffing hierarchy.

A week had gone by since Marilyn had told him to stick his revised org chart up his ass, and that she *absolutely wound not* support it.

Three days ago, the city council conducted a closed-door executive session, not allowing Marilyn or the public to attend, citing sensitive government business. Alice had looked it up in the regs and they were within their rights to do so.

Things had been hush since then.

Until now.

Alice lowered herself into the chair opposite Marilyn's desk. "What do we do?"

"Keep calm, for one thing. Not jump to conclusions."

"But what the hell? Can they really fire me?" The email said the upcoming meeting was to discuss the elimination of the assistant to the mayor position. "Connie Martindale was copied on that email. If human resources is involved, then I'm toast."

"They are not firing you. Just eliminating your position."

"But the result is the same. I have no job. And this is a terrible time in my life for that—divorcing George, and all. I'll have to look for something else immediately, and then how much time can I devote to the campaign?" If Callahan had wanted to push her panic button, he had definitely accomplished that task.

Marilyn lowered her gaze and stared at a document on her desk. "Don't stress yet." She shoved the clipped papers toward Alice. "Read it over. It's the town charter and operating regulations. David is still the city manager, so he leads the council until a new one is appointed. Gale Barker was voted in as the interim city manager at the council meeting the other night. They are within their rights to call us into an emergency meeting."

Alice exhaled. "And on their territory. Not ours."

"Right. Bastards."

She wondered when this "us" against "them" thing had really started. Had it been there all along and they just hadn't seen it? "Seems strange we would meet only with the two of them, and maybe Connie, but not the council, too."

Marilyn screwed up her lips and nodded. "I don't trust this."

The council always met in the town hall, which had a large enough multipurpose room to house a crowd, if needed. Alice didn't think it was an ideal place to hold a meeting that likely would be sensitive, since the room was public and anyone could walk in.

But maybe that's what they wanted?

She glanced at her smartwatch. "It's ten of two. Should we walk over there?"

"In a minute." Marilyn rose and stared out the window. Her gaze seemed to travel the street toward the town hall, on the other side of the city parking lot. "Take your bag, or a briefcase, but don't look too obvious. Be prepared to leave that meeting with whatever personal items you have here, and don't want anyone else to see. If they let you go on the spot, they will not let you back in your office, and someone will box up your things, and you'll have to come get them later."

"That's a little harsh, isn't it?"

"You know that's how it's done." Of course. A disgruntled employee once wiped their computer clean when allowed to return to the office after being terminated.

"Look. We've been careful with the campaign, so I'm feeling okay there. But if there is anything personal..." She met Alice's gaze then. "*Anything personal*, stuff it in your bag. Take your planner. Delete your calendar on your laptop. Take the SIM card out of your work phone and stash it somewhere, but keep the phone too. Leave nothing like that behind."

Alice froze. What the fuck was she saying? "Marilyn? I don't understand."

She faced her. "I have a feeling neither of us will come back to these offices. Now go. Do what I say. I'll take care of shit in here. Be quick, and ready to leave in two minutes."

Alice jerked a nod. *Holy fucking hell.*

She rushed back into her office, her brain rattled. She always kept an oversized tote bag under her desk to carry materials to meetings or to take work home. Grabbing it, she quickly stuffed her planner into it, and a file of contracts for town hall venues she wasn't supposed to have at the office. She found the SIM card on the work phone, slipped it into her bra, then dropped the phone in the bag. She tucked her personal phone into its usual spot in her purse.

Marilyn called out from behind the cracked door. "Ready?"

Shit. No. "Yes."

Quickly, Alice rifled through her desk, pulled out a picture she used to have of George on there, but had slid into the drawer months ago. She tucked that, and another of Ella, into the bag. Glancing about, she decided the rest could wait for the boxing-up person. With a forced exhale, she stared at her laptop for two seconds, then quickly unlocked it from the docking station and slipped it into the bag.

If they asked for it later, she'd give it up.

Eventually.

But she needed time to erase some shit that shouldn't be there.

When they arrived at the town hall and entered the multipurpose room, Alice and Marilyn stood side-by-side facing the back of the room where David Callahan and Gale Barker sat behind the high dais.

Alice swallowed hard and glanced at Marilyn, who stared straight ahead, and then took several determined steps forward.

Alice followed.

"Come on up, ladies. We promise we won't bite."

"How fucking inappropriate," Marilyn hissed under her breath.

She glanced at Alice, narrowing her gaze—then tossed her head back and walked purposefully toward the two men. "What? No chairs for the mayor and her assistant? Where's the pomp and circumstance, and all that, David?" She glanced about. "And where is H.R.? This is a termination meeting. Correct?"

David grinned crookedly and chuckled. "You won't be here long."

"So you say," she remarked.

David looked at Gale, who slid a yellow envelope closer to the edge of the dais. Then he gazed directly at Alice. "Mrs. McBain. Thank you for your loyalty to the citizens of Tuckaway Bay, to the Mayor's office, and to the city council for the past seven years. You have proven your worth and have meticulously done your job. We are sorry to inform you, however, that your position has been eliminated and your services are no longer needed."

Alice's mouth fell slack and she blinked. That was fast. "Excuse me?"

Gale chimed in. "Of course, we have a severance package for you." He tapped the envelope. "It includes health insurance for six months and three months' salary. Should you leave without incident, you can walk away with it today. Thank you for your service to the town."

Alice took a step toward the dais. "I want to speak with someone in Human Resources. That's my right."

Marilyn grasped her arm and held her back. "I should have been consulted on this matter," she said. "She is my assistant. My voice should have been heard."

David lowered his gaze and met hers. "Your voice is irrelevant."

"I disagree."

Both David and Gale stood. "Mayor Morgan, with the utmost respect, we are also here today to request that you tender your resignation and your mayoral duties immediately, effective today. We highly suggest that you hold a press conference this afternoon saying just that, citing your devotion to your senatorial campaign. You will state that as the campaign season heats up, you realize you cannot do both jobs, and do them well, and you do not want the citizens of Tuckaway Bay to suffer because of your career goals. You will do this without question, and you will leave quietly. Unfortunately, we do not offer severance to elected officials."

"I still have a year in my term," she bit out. "The citizens of Tuckaway Bay elected me to this position, and you cannot terminate me without cause. Plus, David, you know what we'd previously discussed. Should I win the Senate, I will resign then. That has always been the plan, and it will remain so." She looked at Alice. "Let's go. We're not discussing any of this further without representation."

They both turned. Callahan halted them with his next words.

"Before you go, perhaps look at these?"

Alice slowly turned back and made eye contact with David. Marilyn continued looking ahead, toward the front of the room. "What is it?" she whispered.

Swallowing hard, Alice stepped forward. David dangled a manila folder over the edge of the dais. "Take a look," he taunted. "It involves both of you."

Trembling, Alice took a few more steps and reached for the folder. Her shaking hands couldn't grasp it though—or perhaps David just let the contents fall—and she watched the images flash before her as they littered the floor at her feet.

She gasped.

Marilyn turned and looked, too. Her face turned whitewash pale.

There they were—she and Marilyn, in black-and-white glossy print—embraced and kissing on the deck of the hotel in Buxton. There were two of them walking hand-in-hand at Virginia Beach last fall. Another, more recently, of them having lunch together, their heads close, at the Grill—and a close-up of Marilyn's bare foot running up Alice's calf under the table. The damning one was of Marilyn kissing Alice in her office. Those were the ones she could see. The others were covered up—and there were many others.

"You bastard." Marilyn stared at the chaos on the floor, then lifted her head and straightened her shoulders. She glared into David's eyes. "This won't work."

"Resign as I strongly suggested, or a similar package of photographs, some more explicit than what you see here, will be delivered to the Tuckaway Bay Gazette, the Charlotte Observer, and the Raleigh News & Observer, plus all Fox News affiliates across the state. They won't publish them as is, but they can certainly report on them. Of course, Slant Politics, the conservative political blog, known for its no-holds-barred policy on posting images and raw footage, will share them in a heartbeat." He looked at Gale. "You have a connection there, don't you?"

Gale grinned and shrugged. "Oh, yeah. My wife's the executive editor."

David nodded. "Once those reach the press, your political career is over, my dear. Probably your marriage, too." He glanced at Alice. "And yours."

Marilyn said nothing—but bent to gather the photos. Alice helped, watching her trembling fingers snatch at the glossy prints. Without another word, she righted herself and gazed cooly at both men. "What are you getting out of this, David? You've already jumped ship to work for Faust. Has he promised you more? Has he placed you on his "play dirty" team? Be careful what you wish because that man is rather slimy. Don't trust him. Oh, but apparently you are slimy, too. Go figure...."

"And your buddy here? Gale? He gets a new job. The council loves your ideas. I'm not in your way, so why get me—*us*—out of the picture?"

David cocked a half-grin. "Frankly, Marilyn, that's no longer any of your concern."

But it suddenly hit Alice. *It's not about Tuckaway Bay.* She stepped forward. "This isn't about the mayor's office or the town council, is it? It's about the Senate. It's about ruining Marilyn's career for good. If you scandalize her now, ruin her reputation locally, then she's out everywhere and for good. Then Fred Faust sails smoothly to his seat at the capitol."

Callahan chuckled and glanced at Gale Barker. "Maybe we should keep her on. Smart cookie. Would you like to be interim mayor, Alice? What about the deputy position?"

"Go fuck yourself." She bent to pick up the last two pictures on the floor.

Gale laughed. "Of course, these tawdry images aside, there's also the other issue."

"What other issue?" Marilyn barked. "What else have you fabricated?"

"Fabricated? Are you insinuating that these pictures are not real?"

"Artificial intelligence can do amazing things these days."

David leaned forward. "But it can't change the fact that you manipulated contracts with the city, so your husband's company got the lion's share of the work around here."

"Or," Gale added, "change the fact that you ordered me to grant zoning permits that shouldn't have been granted."

Marilyn shook her head. "I did no such thing."

He cocked his head. "Oh? Really? What is it you always say, Mayor Morgan, about perception? All we need to do is plant some seeds...."

And she's toast.

Alice blew out a breath.

Marilyn stood stone still, staring at the men. Alice feared she wouldn't be able to budge her.

"Don't you have a resignation to tender, Ms. Morgan?"

Abruptly, Marilyn pivoted and marched steadily toward the exit.

Alice hurriedly followed behind, stuffing the photos into her bag.

"Press conference?" David called out.

Marilyn didn't look back. "Two hours. On my terms. Not yours, David. Now, go be a good boy and go jerk off, or something, with your little mini-me friend there."

If Alice hadn't been so horrified, she might have giggled.

Nine

She gave Marilyn five minutes of silence before talking, because when Marilyn was upset, that's what Alice did. She'd learned that lesson years ago.

They nearly trotted down Main Street, away from the town hall. Marilyn's steps were quick and long, and Alice had difficulty keeping up with her longer stride, especially while lugging the heavy tote bag. After a few minutes, Marilyn halted.

As did Alice.

Her words gushed out like the torrential leading winds of a hurricane while looking directly at Alice. "Call Matt. Tell him to get all the people he can find at the campaign headquarters ASAP. Volunteers. Vacationers. I don't care. I want people. Tell him we are on our way. I want signs. Lots of signs. A big one for the front window and some of those smaller signs on sticks for the people in the crowd to carry. Tell him to get with the printer down the street. They do rush orders.

"Then call the Gazette and tell them we are doing a presser at four this afternoon at the headquarters. Give them the address and see if they will put the word out on social media and the wire services. Do you have a laptop?"

"Yes. I brought the work one. I'm sorry. Did I steal it? I can return, but...."

Marilyn shook her head. "No worries. If they do anything, they won't give you the severance, but don't worry about that. The campaign will cover your salary through the end of the year, or whenever we need to wrap up the official campaign business. We will worry about that later. Get to the headquarters and draft a press release. Send it out immediately after the presser—using your campaign email address, of course. Disconnect the laptop from the government server. Play up the part about me going whole hog into the campaign and that I wish the town of Tuckaway Bay well, and that I promise to always keep my town in mind with anything I shall do in the future." She looked sharply at Alice then. "Play it up, better words. You're good at that."

"I'm on it."

Marilyn reversed course and started back toward the administration building and the mayor's office. "See you soon," she called over her shoulder. "Stay at the campaign headquarters and get that press release done. Help Matt. You know what to do to get ready. I need to resign my fucking job."

And she was off to the races. Literally and figuratively.

Ninety minutes later, Alice watched her lover and the former mayor of Tuckaway Bay give the best damn impromptu campaign speech of her life on the sidewalk of the small coastal town. It was intimate, informal, and powerful. She didn't hover over the crowd, stand on a stump, or hide behind a podium. She stood in the crowd, with the people, microphone in hand, pouring herself, and her campaign points of view, into the dialogue.

And that was exactly what it was—a dialogue. Marilyn held a candid conversation with her constituents about why *she*, and her ideas, were needed in the North Carolina legislature.

Why *she* had to win the Senate seat. And not Fred Faust.

Lia, Julia, Maggie, Belle, and Carol were there, too, cheering along with the others. Alice felt a keen sense of pride at what they had pulled off in less than two hours.

No one walked away from the press conference confused about

where Marilyn Morgan stood on the issues—personally and politically. They knew what her platform was, and why. And, that she would fight like hell—like a mama bear protecting her cubs—for the rights of *all the people* of Tuckaway Bay and the state of North Carolina.

No matter what Fred Faust did, or how he tried to disgrace her campaign.

The people cheered. The press crowded closer, shouting questions. And Alice stood back, Matt at her side, watching and smiling.

Take that, Fred Faust.

And your mini-me, too.

MARILYN THRIVED ON LONG, DEMANDING, AND INSANELY messy days. Pandemonium was her jam. The longer her to-do list, the more disorganized her calendar, the more she loved navigating the insanity. It was like working a puzzle.

And she loved puzzles.

She also loved a challenge. Tell her she can't do something? *Hold my wine.*

But she honestly couldn't remember ever feeling so fatigued, so utterly dog-tired, than she felt right now. She'd had longer days—but never had she lived through a day with as many crests and troughs of stormy emotions as the one she'd just finished.

The hours-long tension coursing throughout her body sent her muscles screaming in discomfort—from the time they'd received the email summons, to the exact moment she saw the photographs scattered on the floor, to the uplifting excitement of the presser, and the moment seconds earlier when she'd silently entered her front door.

The tequila shots at the Grill, after they'd closed down the headquarters for the night, didn't help. While she was never a sloppy drunk—and she wasn't drunk now, just nicely buzzed—she'd been grateful for Matt getting an Uber for both her and Alice. That young man was proving his worth by the hour.

Her head pounded a little, right behind her eyes, radiating toward her temples. Her jaw hurt from clenching her teeth. And smiling.

But the people. *My God. The people were fantastic.*

Nudging off her heels, she dangled them from one hand as she ascended the stairs, making as little sound as possible, and thought about sleeping in the guest room. She wasn't in the mood for Jonathan this evening—she knew a conversation was coming because he'd texted her many times throughout the late afternoon and evening. Texts she'd intentionally ignored.

Sleeping in the guest room would send the wrong signal, though. Not that she was avoiding *him*, but that she was avoiding *the conversation* she knew he wanted to have.

There was a difference, however subtle.

So, she bypassed the spare bedroom and quietly entered the primary suite. A quick glance at their bed, partially lit by the streetlamp outside the window, told her he wasn't there. Before she could react, the lamp in the corner switched on, and her attention drew immediately to her husband, sitting there in a chair.

"Quite the day, I imagine," he said. "You quit your job. You rallied the troops. You ignored my calls."

He sat there poker-faced. Serious. Marilyn was uncertain where this was heading.

Setting her shoes down, she shrugged out of her jacket. "Not the day I expected, but hell, I made it through."

"Impressive press conference. Were you going to share this plan of leaving the mayor's office with me? I thought we were a team." He cocked his head to the side, staring. "Or was what you said the other night just to appease me?"

"No, it wasn't, Jonathan."

"Oh, a knee-jerk reaction, then?"

"Look. It was not a decision I expected to make today," she said.

"I imagine not."

Marilyn exhaled and took her time doing it. "Jonathan, I want to tell you everything that transpired on this hellish and also beautiful day, but honestly...? I'm bushed. Sacked. I can't even think straight right now."

"All that lying has to be exhausting."

"What?"

Jonathan stood. "When did you decide to quit being mayor?"

"I didn't decide. They fired Alice—or rather, let her go, you know, position elimination. The new city manager is in bed with Faust, apparently, which would only have made things more difficult for me. And without Alice, I'm not sure I can run the place, anyway. She was my right hand. It was...ridiculous."

He lifted his chin and studied her. "I imagine losing her was hard."

She hesitated. "Yes."

"So, you quit and made the Senate race your priority." He waited. She said nothing, so he added, "Without talking to me."

"Yes. I did." She unbuttoned the top two buttons on her blouse, meeting his gaze head-on. "It's not like we hadn't explored that option earlier. While they forced my hand on it, honestly, it's probably the best thing."

"And these had nothing to do with your decision?" He thrust a folder toward her.

Panic seized her chest, the sensation squeezing, her breath short. Marilyn stared down at the same type of manila folder that Callahan had shown them earlier—the one that held the pictures. "What's this?"

"I think you know."

"Jonathan...."

"Answer me. These had nothing to do with your decision?"

Shit, shit, shit. "Of course they did." She huffed and turned away, slipping out of her blouse and tossing it on the bench at the foot of the bed. *I can't lose him. I need him.* "I don't want to talk about that right now."

He rushed toward her so quickly, he startled her. Jonathan had never been physical with her, unless in bed, of course, and she was fine with that. But for a moment, seeing him come toward her peripherally, she almost felt frightened. Threatened.

He can ruin your entire career, all your goals and dreams, in mere seconds.

That, was the absolute truth.

"Jonathan, I've been thinking. Maybe you *should* take the job in Texas."

"Oh, no. You don't get to change the subject."

"I'm not. Not really. It's all connected."

He didn't move for several seconds, just stood eyeing her. "You mean to tell me, after everything you've been through today, that you had time to think about me and my job?"

She blinked. "I've been thinking about it since we talked."

"Bullshit." He tossed the envelope at her, and the pictures scattered.

Déjà vu.

Turning away, he ran a hand over his head. "Bull. Shit!"

"Jonathan...."

He whirled back and leaned in closer. "Marilyn, you've tried me for years. You told me you were not seeing other men."

"That was true. I have not seen other men."

"But Alice? What the fuck, sweetheart? I had no clue you needed to scratch that itch. Are you fucking gay? Did you ever plan to tell me about this rather important piece of your perplexing life?"

What he said was true. Her life was a mystery, and she enjoyed hiding the details of how she ticked. She *liked* being the one to decide who got to see *which pieces* of her life—and adored making it difficult for anyone to put the picture fully together.

She was not an open book and never would be—and she *fucking loved* living her life that way.

The only one—the only person in her life who had ever gotten too close—was Jonathan. And their relationship was complicated, at best.

With a sigh, she faced him fully. This day was unraveling much too quickly. "Please calm down. Listen to me."

"No." He pushed a finger toward her face. "Answer me. Are you gay?"

"I'm...bisexual."

"Convenient." He turned and paced toward the window and back, rubbing his hands over his face. "Of course you didn't lie. You didn't have an affair with a man—you suddenly became bisexual so you could get your side-kinks with a woman. Great, Marilyn. Just fucking great."

"It's not like that. Not at all."

He rotated back, glaring. "No. Before you slide into excuse after excuse, I want to know. How long has this been going on?"

Sucking in another breath, she held it in like the secrets she'd been holding for years. Her chest hurt from the strain on her lungs, then she let it out slowly at first, then with a loud and quick whoosh. She closed her eyes. "Over a dozen years."

"You've got to be kidding me."

She opened them again. "No. Maybe a couple of years longer than that. It started when we were working at Bayside."

Jonathan took a few steps closer; his eyes held unspoken questions. "I'm not sure if you realize how deeply that hurts. You've been having an affair, with a woman, for over a decade, and I had no clue. Do you realize how that makes me feel?"

"I'm sorry, Jonathan. It's a part of me I didn't think you needed to know. It's not us. It's something different."

He glared. "It's not us. Right."

"You and I—we have a different kind of relationship than what I have with Alice. And vice versa."

"Normal people don't get to do that, Marilyn, compartmentalize their lives. People running for government office don't either."

"Sure, they do. They do it all the time."

"And that gets them into trouble. People expect transparency. There's nothing transparent about hiding who you are."

She scowled at him for a moment, then shook her head. How dare he accuse her of hiding? She damn well knew who she was. "Because they're not smart about it. I can keep things separate, Jonathan. I have for a long time. I can live in two worlds."

"Well, I can't. I don't want you in two worlds. I want you in my world, only. It needs to stop now. End it."

"I... I'm not sure I can, Jonathan. She's been part of my life for so long and..." *Am I unraveling? What the fuck. I don't unravel.*

He can ruin your entire career, all your goals and dreams, in mere seconds.

He edged closer, looking directly into her eyes. "Listen to me, Marilyn. I'm not moving to fucking Texas. Getting me out of your way might seem the right thing to do, but it's not. You need me here. I'm staying. In fact, I'm all in."

She shook her head. "I don't understand."

"I'm not going anywhere, and you aren't either."

"But," she countered, "if you go to Texas, then you'll be spared of anything ugly should it happen. Jonathan, there is so much we need to discuss, but maybe it would be easier if we just weren't together right now."

"Are you saying a separation? Isn't that political suicide?"

"But that's where the job comes in."

"Right. It's a handy excuse."

"I don't know. Maybe." It was never what she'd wanted, but suddenly, she was feeling backed into a corner. *Fight or flight?*

"Naw. No. Sweetheart, my leaving is not the answer. You need me. You have a Senate race to win. And whether or not you think about it much, I believe in your platform and why you are running. I'm behind all that one hundred percent. You will make an excellent senator. This state needs you, but..." Bending, he picked up a handful of pictures off the floor. "But this is why you need me—to put this to rest."

He edged closer. "I love you. I've always loved you. And from this moment on, I'm going to be by your fucking side for every minute of your campaign, supporting you and showing the entire goddamn state of North Carolina my commitment to you, whether or not you want me there. Got it?"

His navy-blue eyes bored into hers. "And if I'm by your side, she won't be."

"She's my campaign manager. I have to work with her."

"Not if you fire her. Didn't you tell me you hired someone new a couple of weeks ago?"

Shit. "Matt? He's not ready. I need Alice."

Narrowing his gaze, he glared. "Tread softly, Marilyn. Right now, with this, you are not holding the cards."

He is not fucking doing this.

Oh, but he is.

Too tired to think, too exhausted to fight back, too confused give a damn, she simply agreed. "All right. All right, Jonathan. You win." *For now.*

"Good. Let's get some sleep." He turned toward the bed, tugging at his T-shirt.

"Jonathan?"

He glanced her way.

"I need to do something first. Trust me?"

"What is it?"

"Something I need to finish."

He held her gaze momentarily.

"I won't be long."

He nodded. "Go. Get it out of your system."

Right.

As if I could.

Years earlier....

ALICE TOOK ANOTHER DRINK OF HER BOURBON AND grimaced. Drinking alone was overrated. Honestly, she should get home to Ella.

George was out of town at a teacher's convention, so she had arranged for a sitter for a few hours after work. Home was honestly the last place she wanted to be. She had things to work out.

So unlike her. What was this woman doing to her brain?

But Marilyn was nowhere to be found. Where she was right now. And it hadn't been her intent to find her. That's why she'd chosen this hole-in-the-wall bar. Definitely not a Marilyn kind of place.

She'd wanted downtime. Alone time. To think.

And honestly, she wanted to numb herself a little.

Part of that *was* because of Marilyn, who had made the comment about Alice being a dull girl. She was right. *I am a dull girl.* And she'd been absolutely fine with that for a long time. She had Ella, and she had George. They were her family, her light, and her life. If anything, they made her shine, and that was all she needed.

Right?

But the other part about needing downtime kept poking at her—Alice couldn't get Marilyn out of her mind.

She couldn't stop thinking about how soft her fingertips were, gliding over her shoulders and neck muscles. She couldn't erase the seductive wisp of her voice, which wound around her like a curl of smoke. Tempting. Teasing her.

So, she broke the routine. Got a sitter.

Went day drinking. Hell, she was so out of touch with the bar scene—when did day drinking cut off and night drinking begin? Happy hour?

It seemed like a good idea.

The bar sat down the road from work and was basically a local joint with a beachy vibe. Vacationers rarely dropped in, or so she'd heard. She'd only been there once, when she and George had a date night and felt like doing something different, out-of-character.

She chose it because, honestly, her life felt like it was spinning out of control, and maybe out-of-character would make her feel less dull.

Her now empty glass rattled with cubes and reeked of whiskey. Her head fuzzy, she tipped the glass toward Sam, the bartender. "Another, please." Smiling, she met his gaze. They'd exchanged names early on.

He shook his head. "Last one for a while, Alice, so maybe not shoot it back. And have some peanuts." He slid the bowl of nuts closer to her.

"Sure thing."

She'd humor him for a while. Yeah, nurse it. Right. She wasn't driving anyway, so who cared? She'd call a cab. Or have him do it.

Yeah. Her brain was super-fuzzy right now, and driving was not on the agenda for the evening.

She fished her car keys out of her purse and handed them to him. "Put those somewhere, okay?" *Probably the smartest thing I'll do tonight.*

Sam smiled and took the keys. He was handsome for an older guy. And in a time pre-George, she might have been attracted. Or even tempted. She didn't know exactly what it was about him, maybe it was because he had a dick.

Lately, she didn't seem to be interested in dicks.

Isn't that the point?

She should be, though, right? Interested? Maybe she should try to seduce him. Prove to herself she's not gay.

Alice sat up a little straighter. *What the hell am I thinking?*

Sam took her empty glass and replaced it with a full one. She smiled at him in defiance, tipped up the glass, and downed the straight liquor. That action immediately accelerated her buzz. Hearing a burst of shouting, she glanced behind her, her head swimming a little, as a crowd of people shoved through the door—three cocky dicks followed by one sweet pussy.

Pussy. Shit.

Marilyn.

No.

I am in no frame of mind for her. What the hell is she doing here?

Sometimes she wondered if it was all in her head. Marilyn was all subtle innuendo, and she stoked an uncomfortable desire within Alice whenever she was near. Uncomfortable only because it was foreign, she guessed. She supposed she was battling a little inside herself...being attracted to a woman.

She couldn't say for certain if Marilyn was a lesbian. Maybe she was bisexual. There were rumors. *I can't explain why I'm attracted to her.*

Because I am.

And fighting it.

She glanced at Sam, who was busy serving up drinks. She should call a cab soon.

"Fancy seeing you here, Alice. I thought that was your car outside. This seat taken?"

Yeah, fancy that.

Alice's gaze shifted to the mirror behind the bar.

Marilyn looked directly at her in the reflection.

"No." She stood. "Never expected to see you in this kind of place."

"Must be fate."

Sure, a chance encounter. Right.

"I'm on my way out, Marilyn. Sorry. See you at the office." She nodded toward Sam. "Call that cab now?"

He gave her a wave and reached for his cell.

Alice avoided looking at Marilyn and turned away.

But Marilyn caught her wrist. "Alice..." She dragged out her name, like a song from a siren's mouth. *Dammit.*

She made direct eye contact. "Have to pee before the cab comes. I'm a little too drunk to...."

To what? Face my attraction to you?

She pulled out of Marilyn's grasp and stumbled to the women's restroom. Locating a stall, she stepped inside and closed the door, leaning into it. *Safe in here.* Her cheek rested against the cool metal. She didn't need to pee. Did she? Wasn't sure. Just needed to get away.

"I practically ran from her."

Insane. This was insane. Likely, Marilyn had no interest in her whatsoever. Stupid, stupid, dull girl.

Pushing back from the door, she stood for a second and gathered her wits. The cab should be there soon, so she made a plan. *Walk out, go straight through the bar, and into the cab. No eye contact. No conversation.*

She left the stall and looked at her reflection in the bathroom mirror.

"Hello, Alice." Marilyn stepped around the corner.

The breath whooshed out of her. "Marilyn...."

She sank against the sink, suddenly exhausted. Of what? The day? Too much bourbon? Fighting her infatuation?

Suddenly, Marilyn stood behind her—*too close and not close enough*—her face beside Alice's. She could feel her soft skin against her cheek and savored the sound of her even breaths. Their gazes held each other in the reflection.

"When are you going to stop running from me, huh?" Her voice came to her on a whisper, low and wispy. "You work so hard, Alice, and are way too stressed. You take it all so seriously."

She's right. I do. "But I have to take work seriously. It's what I do."

Swiftly, Marilyn grasped her and twisted their bodies so they were facing each other now, staring into each other's eyes. Alice found that a little more difficult than meeting her stare in the mirror—but also more intense.

Marilyn traced her lower lip with a forefinger. "Shh. Not now. No talk of work."

"Then what?"

"This."

She didn't rush. Didn't push too close. She simply leaned in, touched her nose against Alice's, barely hesitated, and then kissed her.

For the briefest moment, her world stopped—then her head spun. Kissing soft lips, a woman's lips, *Marilyn's lips*, was different. They were plump and smooth, soft. At first, the kiss was slow, seductive, a mind-bending tease of touches and nips. But the intensity increased as Marilyn dragged her mouth over Alice's in such a way that she knew Marilyn meant to claim. And when she stopped, only for a heartbeat, her tongue slipped inside Alice's mouth, mingling with hers, and sending her into a downward spiral of carnal decadence.

Alice gripped the sink.

The sensation of the kiss shot through her like a foreign entity.

Exciting. Desired. Terrifying.

Marilyn shifted and let out a hard moan, aligning the lengths of their bodies, breasts crowding into each other. Alice's nipples reacted, tingled, and she knew they were pebble hard.

"Let me ease the tension, Alice." Her breath was hot against her neck. "Let me. You know there is something between us...."

Something. Yes. No.

"Marilyn. No. I'm...."

She pulled back. "You're what?"

"Married."

"This is between us, Alice. No one else. It's okay to take care of your needs."

Needs? I need this?

Confused at the pleasure she felt and her warped sense of sensuality, coupled with a bourbon-induced haze, Alice couldn't figure out what she should or shouldn't be feeling. Part of her wanted to relax and go with the flow. The other part wanted to fight, push her away, be appalled.

Marilyn's hand fell to her hip and then moved to her thigh. She bunched up her skirt in her fist.

Alice exhaled hard. "Shit."

Attracted. I am. To you.

Something unleashed inside her. Deepened the haze. Alice leaned forward and grasped a lock of Marilyn's hair in each hand, threading the length through her fingers. Pulling her close, she kissed her again, deeper this time, urging a response. Marilyn's hands grappled lower, gathering Alice's skirt up around her thighs. A fingertip lazily dragged over her panties, sending Alice into a shivering mass of sensation.

Marilyn tugged her closer with her other arm. "I want to touch you." Her fingers slipped beneath the sheer fabric. "I want to feel your heat."

Alice leaned into her, caught between the sink and Marilyn's body. Gasping, she clutched her, their mouths playing, tasting. Then, Marilyn's finger dipped further into her panties.

I might die. "Marilyn."

"Shh. No talk. Not now. Lean on me."

Alice laid her head on Marilyn's shoulder, eyes closed, blocking out everything but her probing finger and within seconds—

The intensity of a swift, consuming, and deeply erotic orgasm shattered her.

She bit into Marilyn's shoulder.

Marilyn held her close. After a moment, she straightened her panties and skirt, then tipped Alice's face upward to meet her gaze. She searched deep into her eyes for an uncomfortable length of time.

Alice abruptly pushed off the sink. She dodged Marilyn, stumbling toward the door, pausing only for a second and risking a backward glance.

God, she is beautiful.

Then she raced for the cab.

Ten

Get it out of my system. Sure.

If Jonathan only knew how impossible that was.

Marilyn left him, left their bedroom and their home, and drove to the other side of Tuckaway Bay. Her buzz was gone, fully jolted back to awareness by his declarations. Life was going to get even more serious.

It had already been one helluva day.

Taking her car, not wanting to call another Uber, she avoided any record of where she'd been this evening.

Turning into the subdivision, she slowed her speed. She'd driven by Alice's home many times prior to this but had only been there once before.

Tonight was different.

She parked on the road, headed up the sidewalk, stepped onto the wide porch, and knocked.

After a moment, Alice opened the interior door and stared out through the screen. "What are you doing here?"

"May I come in?"

Alice glanced past Marilyn, like she didn't know what to do. "You don't come here, Marilyn. Why?"

"I know." Pausing, she looked back at the dark street. "Alice, please? We need to talk."

She rarely said *please*. Even rarer, that she'd start any discussion with the word. But tonight, she wasn't above begging.

"Sure." Alice unlocked the door.

Marilyn slipped inside and rushed past her, the words tumbling out. "What are we going to do if those pictures get out? I don't trust Callahan." They'd avoided that subject all afternoon and evening until now.

Alice followed her with a shrug. "Deny? Claim they are artificial intelligence? I don't know."

Marilyn whirled back. "That's not a bad idea. The A.I. angle."

"Do you think it will come to that?"

Marilyn strolled further into the house, Alice behind her. She slowed and rotated when she got to the living room. "It's been a long time. I picture your house in my head, looking just like this. It's you," she whispered.

Feelings of remorse quickly washed over her. She'd only been there once before, and that was a shame. She and Alice had put their lives on such strict hold that they truly hadn't gotten to know each other better on a simple, down-home basis. For that, she was sorry.

But she wouldn't tell her that. Not tonight. Not yet.

Alice ambled toward her, stopping only to turn out a lamp on a side table. Now, the room was lit only with the low light from the entry hall. "How long can you stay?" she whispered.

Marilyn sighed and reached for her, jerking her closer. "For a while," she murmured. Her lips were now dangerously close to the tender spot right behind Alice's ear. She knew that with one swipe of the tip of her tongue, she could send her into pre-orgasmic shudders.

But she'd promised Jonathan.

I don't give a fucking shit about Jonathan at the moment. I can live in two worlds, no matter what he says, and I want to be in this one. In this house. I cannot give Alice up—even for him.

"Marilyn...?"

She stepped back, searching Alice's eyes. "I have some news."

"Oh?"

"I'm afraid I have to let you go. From the campaign. Matt will take over."

The stunned look on Alice's face was almost her undoing. Why was she doing this? Putting her through this? Them? Was it all so that Jonathan would stick around and make her world appear perfect? To her constituents? Or, was he forcing this because he loved her and didn't want to lose her?

Obviously, he was messing with her head. And no one messed with her head like Jonathan.

Alice took a breath. "What are you saying?"

"Jonathan has copies of the pictures. He wants me to fire you."

"Shit." Alice pushed back, putting space between them. "You've got to be kidding me. Losing two jobs in one day was definitely not on my bingo card."

"I know. I'm sorry."

"How did Jonathan get the pictures?"

Marilyn sighed and turned, arms crossed, pacing a few steps back and forth. "Honestly, I didn't ask him that question, but I can only assume it's Callahan. They were in the same type of folder."

"Callahan is a bastard."

"I'd say that's being kind."

Alice grasped Marilyn's elbow and stopped her pacing. "What do you want to do?"

"Well, obviously, I don't want to let you go."

Closing the gap between them again, Alice crowded closer. "Then don't. Because your husband suddenly grew balls, you're going to bend the knee to him?"

Who is this woman? Marilyn chuckled. "Who else grew balls?"

Alice grinned and reached for her hand. "Come to bed," she whispered. "I want you in my bed."

"Shit, Alice," she hissed.

She led her toward the hall and stairwell. "Come."

"He's going to watch me like a hawk. Us. He's going to watch us so closely."

Alice halted and looked over her shoulder, smiling. "Everyone is watching us closely. We have to be careful. For you, for the campaign, for us. This could be our last night together for a while—but we can play the game until it's over. Right? Until we are finally together?"

She looked at her with such sincerity, and suddenly, for the first time in their relationship, Marilyn wondered if she was only now truly seeing Alice for who she was.

"I love you, Marilyn," she whispered.

Her heart twisted a little. "I love you too, sweetheart."

"We can do this."

We can. *I can.* "Yes. Absolutely. Take me to your bed."

THE NEXT MORNING, ALICE LAZILY BLINKED AWAKE, FULLY aware of Marilyn spooning her from behind. Her slim arms wrapped around her, clasped together at her waist, were like a warm, safe hug. Marilyn's even breathing told her she was still sleeping, and Alice hated to wake her, but would need to soon.

Her car was still in the drive, and the dusky dawn wouldn't last much longer.

Would this be their future? Waking up together every morning, their bodies entwined, breathing in sync, heartbeats echoing off each other? She'd longed for this, prayed for this, and had even caused heartache, just for moments like this one.

Was it worth it? Was this their destiny?

"Alice..." Marilyn whispered her name.

"Yes?"

"I should go."

She nodded, looking toward the streaks of dawn filtering through the filmy curtains at the window. "I know."

With a deep sigh, Marilyn pulled away and rolled onto her back. Alice did the same but slightly faced her. "Your car."

"Yes." Marilyn stared at the ceiling.

Alice watched her chest rise and fall, taking in and releasing a couple of cycles of breath. "I love having you here," she murmured.

Marilyn faced her. "This is something that should have happened long ago, and not just because I'm, or we're, having a crisis. This is too special for that." She searched Alice's eyes. "If I have any regrets, it's that."

Alice eased out a slow breath. "No talk of regrets. It makes me feel like we're ending things."

She shook her head. "No, Alice. I don't see it that way."

Then how do you see it? "Then what?"

Marilyn propped herself up on an elbow, angling toward her. "Sweetheart, we need to figure something out. Jonathan won't have you traveling with me, being my right-hand girl any longer. He plans to stick to me like glue. So, like you said last night, this might be it for a while. Until after the election."

Alice stared ahead, looking deep into her eyes. "You love him. Don't you?"

She didn't linger in her response. "I've loved him since we were children. He understands me. He's supported me. He's, basically, my best friend. Our lives, and the lives of our families, are intertwined." She paused, holding her gaze. "I don't see Jonathan not being a part of my life, Alice. Can you handle that?"

Suddenly, she felt very confused. "What are you saying?"

Her eyelids closed briefly, then opened wide. "What I'm saying, darling, is that as much as I love waking up next to you like this, in a bed that would be our own, in a room that would be our own, in a house of our own... We have to be prepared, knowing that possibly that won't happen for a very long time."

The warm-fuzzies of moments earlier were suddenly gone—stripped from her heart and soul. She'd thought they were getting closer.

Reality, though, was fickle. And sucked.

She'd waited years for the perfect moment that would likely never come.

How had she been so gullible?

YEARS EARLIER....

. . .

JUST OUT OF THE SHOWER—WHERE SHE'D ATTEMPTED TO wash the bar, the smell of whiskey, and the lingering essence of Marilyn from her body—the doorbell rang. Alice glanced at the clock in the bedroom, briefly fluffed her damp hair with a towel, and slipped into her kimono-style bathrobe. It was after ten o'clock. Who would come by at this late hour?

She considered not answering the door when the bell rang a second time.

"Well, all right," she hissed, quickly pulling a comb through her tangles. She didn't want the doorbell to wake Ella up. Tightening the robe's belt, she padded down the stairs and pulled the sheer curtain away from the sidelight.

She froze and momentarily thought about running back upstairs.

Instead, she flipped on the entry light, unlatched the door, and pulled it open. She didn't turn on the porch light because she could see well enough with the light from the hall.

Marilyn stood on the front porch, framed by the screen door. "We need to talk."

She looked out-of-place standing there, Alice thought, but stunning. Her blond hair cascaded over her left shoulder, reflecting the creamy moonlight. Her red lips invited temptation. And her eyes spoke, no, pleaded to be let inside.

"Not a good time, Marilyn. We can talk tomorrow at the office."

A corner of her mouth curled up. "This is not appropriate office conversation. It's rather private. I think you know that. Your husband is out of town, right?"

Alice glanced over her shoulder, toward the stairwell. Might as well tell her. "Yes, he's at a conference. How did you know?"

"I heard you mention it earlier to someone."

"But my daughter is here, upstairs sleeping."

Marilyn glanced beyond her. "How old is she?"

"Just turned five."

"I'm sure she's lovely. Just like her mother."

Alice's cheeks heated. "She is beautiful. Not that she gets it from me, though."

Marilyn stepped closer to the screen door. "I think you're so very pretty, Alice. Inside and out. Can we talk?"

Those eyes again. Their sea-green hue seized her soul deep. With a sigh, she flicked the latch on the screen door and motioned her inside.

Shit. Moment of truth?

What *is* the truth?

The door closed. Their gazes skidded sideways as Marilyn moved into the entry and turned toward the living room. She took a step inside.

Alice halted at the arched opening, half-turned into the room. "I was about to get some water," she said. "May I get you something?"

Marilyn said nothing but gently shook her head.

Alice rotated toward the hall then, intending to head for the kitchen, but halted. Her back muscles crawled with sensation.

"Alice, look at me."

Closing her eyes, she gave herself a moment—one cleansing breath—and then turned back.

Marilyn stood inches away. "What I would like," she said softly, "is for you to slow down and stop running from me. I can chase for a while, but eventually, I'll get frustrated and find other prey."

Prey? "I didn't know I was prey."

"Figure of speech."

"No. No. What do you mean by that, Marilyn?" *Because, honestly, prey is exactly how you make me feel. I just hadn't put the word to it yet.*

She drew closer. "Alice. I've been sending subtle—and maybe not so subtle—messages for a couple of weeks now. I'm extremely attracted to you. I want—"

"I'm married. I have a husband."

She nodded. "So do I."

That surprised Alice. She didn't know. "I'm not gay."

Marilyn's chin lowered, and she fixed her gaze on Alice's face. One corner of her glossy red lips turned up into a sexy smirk. "I'm bi."

"I assumed."

"And you are...?"

"Confused." She tilted her chin.

"Because you are attracted to me?"

"Yes."

"And you are curious?"

"About sex without a penis? Yes."

Laughter escaped Marilyn's lips. Her hands went about Alice's waist and tugged. "My sweet Alice," she whispered, her eyes searching. "You are a gem. An innocent, delightful gem. I assure you, darling, that I can make up for the lack of a penis."

Well, that is intriguing. "I'm sure you are quite...capable. I...."

Marilyn drew back and stared. "Alice. I want you. I need you to know I don't do this casually. I have feelings for you, in addition to a very strong sexual attraction."

"Feelings." Alice scoffed. "You barely know me."

"I know enough."

"Marilyn, I... Look. What happened in the bar? Shouldn't have happened."

She placed a finger on Alice's lips, exactly as she had done in the bar earlier. "Shh, my sweet. Don't overthink. It causes the brain to send messy signals to the heart."

My heart. My heart is not my concern at the moment. Her female parts were going wacky with Marilyn's nearness.

"Come." Marilyn grasped her hand. "Let's sit and talk."

She pulled her toward the sofa and they sank into it. Marilyn's arm settled around Alice's back. Involuntarily, Alice leaned against her shoulder.

Marilyn stroked the backs of her fingertips over her cheek.

"You're a hard worker, Alice," she whispered. "You rush to be better than the next person. Nothing wrong with working hard if you let yourself play some, too." She paused, threading her fingers through Alice's damp hair. "The stress will eat you up if you let it."

She was right. She knew that.

But this wasn't about stress. It was about something else entirely.

"My husband knows nothing about my needs beyond our marriage. I keep it all very separate. And I am very discreet. We can make this work, Alice."

What was she suggesting? That she keeps her life intact and dabbles in occasional Marilyn dalliances on the side?

"I don't want to talk about it." Talking would only screw things up. What she wanted at that moment was for Marilyn to continue playing with her hair, and caress her face a little longer. Feel her warmth.

"We don't have to talk."

"Hold me?" She slipped her arms around Marilyn's waist, and Marilyn tucked her into her body.

"You smell heavenly." Marilyn said a few moments later.

Alice had drifted off, dozed, apparently still under the influence of the hot shower, a bit of lingering bourbon, and caressing fingertips. Marilyn's lips were dangerously close to her ear, and she remained still, savoring the sensation of her steady breath against her damp skin, enjoying the nearness of her mouth.

Her breathing came in rhythm.

In. Out... In. Out.

Like a heartbeat.

Steady and certain. Steady and certain.

Determined.

Alice shifted and angled her face upward. Their mouths brushed. Marilyn's hand abandoned the shock of hair she'd been stroking and clutched the back of her head. Alice sank further into the sofa and Marilyn's embrace.

They kissed.

Marilyn's lips were velvety warm and tasted like cinnamon. A ribbon of something foreign—something wild and sensual and free— uncoiled behind Alice's breastbone. It sizzled and popped and sprang to life as the kiss deepened. She responded with urgency—wanted to open up her chest and take her inside. She loved the way Marilyn made her feel.

Her body was on fire, like an unbridled electrical current.

Like being held at bay for too long—perhaps a lifetime?—and was now unexpectedly, gleefully, fiercely set free.

Free.

"Such a wicked little fox," Marilyn breathed, pulling the sash of Alice's robe away from her waist, the sides falling open. She gazed languidly at Alice's body. "Lovely," she murmured.

Alice moaned.

"Yes, my sweet...."

Marilyn zipped the sash from her robe. "This may make things easier. And interesting."

Alice opened her eyes and realized Marilyn was about to blindfold her. Gently, she covered her eyes and tied the sash snug at the side of her head.

"Okay?"

She nodded. *Yes. I am definitely okay.*

The blindfold was a pleasant touch. Not knowing what would happen next. Forced to wait. Anticipate. Let it happen. Out of her control.

Nice.

She could wonder. Imagine. Feel.

Marilyn wants me.

I want her.

Alice didn't want to be in control. She no longer wanted to be the woman in charge. Didn't want to be the caretaker, the fixer, the mother hen. Wanted someone else be the boss, take over.

Gone was the goody-two-shoes nice girl. At least for the moment.

"Please...?" *Is pleading what she wants?*

"Alice...? Are you sure?"

Her body hummed in response. "Don't make me wait."

She couldn't see. Could only feel. The delay was killing her.

Marilyn's breath whispered against her hipbone.

Her thigh.

Quick, even pants escaped her throat. Alice wanted to lurch forward, grasp her, but was hesitant. Desire roiled deep inside her belly, aching to be unleashed.

Shuddering, she clutched at the kimono, balling it up in her fists.

But then Marilyn pulled away. A cool breeze from the air conditioner wafted over Alice's exposed body. The sensation felt surreal, distorted, disengaged....

She tugged the sash from her eyes.

Marilyn stood beside the sofa. "I have to go, sweetheart," she whispered.

Alice pushed into a sitting position. *But I want more.* "Why?"

"I am leaving you to think. Before we go any further, before I invest myself—before you make this kind of commitment—I want to be certain. Both of us need to be certain."

Shit. "Marilyn, I don't understand." Alice was confused...and hurt?

"We need to know how deep we can take this, Alice. How far exactly are you willing to go with this relationship?"

"Are you serious? We can't have a relationship. We're both married."

Marilyn caught Alice's gaze, holding the stare for an uncomfortable length of time. "Good night, Alice," she finally said. "Sleep, and we'll talk soon."

"When?"

Lowering her chin, she gazed into Alice's eyes. "Soon."

Eleven

"Matt? Would you look at this contract? Did you sign off on this?"

Alice glanced over her shoulder into the buzz of the campaign headquarters. *Where the hell is he, anyway?* He was there just a few minutes ago, having arrived back in Tuckaway Bay a few hours before Marilyn was due.

It was August, and they'd been busy as shit for the past six weeks. With Marilyn crisscrossing the state hosting town halls, attending events, kissing babies, and navigating impromptu drop-ins to small-town eateries and local business establishments, their days were sliding by fast and furious.

Which was totally fine with Alice. It kept her focused on the campaign, and not on her crumbling relationship with Marilyn. Frankly, she wasn't exactly sure where that stood, at the moment. Marilyn was all-in focused on the campaign.

As she should be, at this stage of the game.

Most times when Marilyn rolled into a new town, she was a welcome visitor. The people liked her fresh take on controversial views that the state's residents and legislature had haggled over for decades. Occasionally, they'd encounter a few ultra-conservative Faust fans—but had avoided any kind of tussle where they were concerned.

She and Marilyn had barely seen each other since the campaign hit the road. The compromise Marilyn made with her husband was that Matt traveled with them, not Alice. Jonathan took leave from his job until after the election, so he could be at his wife's side.

Alice stayed back and manned the headquarters. That's how she got to keep her job.

It wasn't ideal, but she agreed it was the safest and most logical decision—for many reasons. Miraculously, the images of her and Marilyn hadn't surfaced publicly—but that didn't mean they could let their guard down.

Not at all.

And they were ready if Faust, or his minions, played dirty.

She scanned the room again for Matt. Hadn't he just been there moments ago?

Volunteers lined the far wall at tables, stuffing envelopes and handwriting notes to potential local voters. The call center, in the middle of the room, was the epicenter of their efforts—where staff monitored the phones, answered and sent email from the public, and fact-checked social media posts. In the back of the space, they'd carved out a more secluded area, quiet and private, separated by a large floor-to-ceiling room partition. A few well-trained volunteers worked on donor strategies there, as well as drafting emails to established supporters, and writing enticing copy to those who were interested, but had not yet committed.

The activity in the room looked and sounded like chaos—but it was far from it.

Matt had created a well-tuned machine. He had a process for everything and delegated well. He also had a knack for choosing the right volunteers for exactly the right duties, and was a whiz at organizing both Marilyn and herself—all hefty tasks. He'd fashioned an aggressive schedule to run them right up to the debate in September and then sail on toward the vote—and the win—in early November.

While Alice had worked hard to set a positive tone within the campaign headquarters, and with their volunteer staff, she was damn certain that when Marilyn landed the senate seat, Matt deserved the lion's share of the credit.

They couldn't have pulled it all off without him.

"Matt? Anyone seen him?"

No response.

Rising, she stepped further into the drone. The energy created by the glut of campaign business hit her full force as she moved through the room—phones ringing, people chatting, the T.V. in the corner blaring MSNBC news.

The door to the street opened, and she glanced that way, hoping to see Matt. But Griff, from the coffee shop down the street, pushed through the door instead, carrying a couple of coffee trays. Two of his employees trailed behind carrying more of the same, plus three boxes of donuts.

Alice rushed forward and took the tray from Griff. "You, my friend, are a lifesaver." She nodded to a staffer close by and handed her the tray. "Can you help them get all this to the back of the room? Let's clear a table."

The woman nodded and glanced at the coffee-and-donut carriers. "Sure. This way."

Griff plucked up the larger-sized cup in the tray's corner before she left. "This one's yours, Alice. Specially made. Can't let you go without caffeine."

"Ah. Mocha is my jam." She smiled back. "You are sweet. You always remember."

"Always. When have I ever forgotten your order?"

"Never." She took her cup and quickly sipped, then sighed. "You're a good friend, Griff, and I thank you. Seriously, your coffee is the best."

The guy smiled through his scruffy gray beard and mustache. She'd always thought he had a pleasant smile—but honestly, she'd never noticed the light blue color of his eyes before now. Almost gray.

Must be the lighting in here.

"I like to help out," he said.

She blinked and glanced away from him, again scanning the space for Matt. Had he left?

Griff went on. "Besides, you, Marilyn, and this entire crew are doing the good work."

"Well, we appreciate that." She took a quick sip of the mocha. "God, that's good. Even if there was a way I could inject this directly into my veins, I wouldn't, because three-quarters of the experience is the pleasure it gives my mouth." Her cheeks immediately heated.

Griff arched a brow.

Shit. She was in no way sending out sexual innuendo. "I mean, my tongue."

He laughed.

Shit. Shit! "Taste buds?"

"Maybe you should stop while you're ahead."

This time, she was the one to laugh out loud. "Duly noted. But seriously, we appreciate the coffee and goodies. Now, give me the bill."

Griff waved his hands. "No bill. On the house. I want to support the campaign."

"Well, we appreciate that, but you are a small business, so please, Griff, send me a bill. In fact, how about if we make a deal? Every Monday you bring coffee and goodies, like today, to get us started on the week, you leave a bill, and we pay you. See how that works?"

"I have a different proposition."

"That really wasn't a proposition, Griff."

"Oh, but it sounded like one to me."

"Wrong. Just business."

"Well, then." He paused, taking a step back, his gaze narrowed. "I propose we discuss this business deal over a glass of wine tonight after closing hours."

"Ha! Your closing hours or mine?" She never knew what time she'd leave for the day.

"Whatever works. I close at four, but I know you are here much later. And I have a bottle of wine I've been holding back for a special occasion. So, how about whenever you close for the evening, you walk the three blocks down Main Street to my shop, knock on the door, and then we can continue this nonsensical paying-for-coffee conversation?"

Alice stared at him for a couple of heartbeats. "Your words, sir, are confusing."

"They are?"

"Yes."

"Then let me make this simpler." He took a couple of steps and leaned closer. "Wine. Tonight. My place. On your way home."

Shit. He's asking me out. "I... Uh." She glanced about nervously, then settled her gaze on his face. "Griff. Are you asking me for a date?"

"I'm asking my friend to share a bottle of wine."

"You know I'm married." She wanted to put that out there, even though....

Griff didn't mince words. "Alice McBain, word on the street is that you're separated. That George is living in the mountains for the summer, and that you two are on the verge of a divorce."

Not sure what to say, she stammered. "I... Well, the thing is..." How did anyone know? "Wow."

"It's a small town, Alice."

"Apparently smaller than I realized."

"So what do you say?"

She couldn't. She loved counting Griff as a friend, but that was as far as it would ever go. "You know, this place buzzes throughout the night some days, and while Marilyn is traveling, we try to get a lot done, so I'm not exactly sure... Did you say a special bottle of wine?"

"I did. And now you're rambling."

"Right."

She bit her lip. All of this was rather unexpected. Griff was hitting on her? Oh boy. Wait until the girls get that bit of news.

But they really needed to talk. She needed to let him know that no matter what the local rumor mill insisted, she was still unavailable. "Look. Griff, that sounds really nice—"

"I hear a but coming."

"Yes. But I need to take a rain check."

"Of course, Alice." His grin fading, he glanced toward the door. "Seems my crew has left without me. Enjoy the mocha."

"I will. Thank you." She tipped the cup toward him, worried at his abrupt leaving. Had she screwed up? Insulted him?

But as he passed, he paused at her shoulder. "Just in case you've forgotten," he said softly, "a rain check means there is a next time. The invitation is open, and the ball is in your court." He headed for the door.

Alice stared after him. The room fell silent. People still hustled around her, and their mouths still moved like they were talking, but there was no sound. It was all drowned out by the disturbing scream in her head shouting: *What the fuck just happened here?*

SEVERAL HOURS LATER, MARILYN BREEZED INTO THE headquarters. Even though it was late, volunteers were still working—until she stepped through the door and everything halted. They rushed to greet her with offers of coffee, water, and the latest news. Matt had trained them well.

Marilyn was their rock star.

Alice stood back, watching her work the small crowd with laughter, hugs, and handshakes. She thanked them for their diligent efforts and their loyalty, tossed a quick smile at Alice, and then returned her full attention to the staff.

She was never down. The woman never took off her game face.

Matt met her about halfway through the space, and then they headed for the war room, a separate office near the back of the old store. They often used it for strategizing, and for private meetings. Their heads tipped toward each other as they talked and walked.

They've gotten close while on the road. For a moment, Alice felt a twinge of jealousy, then shook it off.

Ridiculous.

Matt had arrived back at the headquarters not long after Griff left, and they'd settled the issue on the town hall contract for Wilmington the week after the debate, the first week of September. What Matt had agreed to was a mistake, and he'd handled it easily with a call to the local media there.

But he'd been evasive. Elusive. About it all, and about where he'd been.

Maybe I'm just paranoid.

Maybe I need a break.

Since then, she'd wandered about aimlessly, chatting, checking up on progress for this and that, and cleaned off the coffee and donut table.

What the fuck? Am I bored?

I'm something.

What she was, if she cared to admit it, was lonely.

Ever since Griff had left earlier in the day, she'd felt discombobulated, and if she were honest with herself, insecure.

It had been years since any man had approached her with romantic interest. She and George had been married for over two decades, and until she'd met Marilyn, she was totally committed to their relationship. And after Marilyn—even though that was an indiscretion—she had not been tempted to cheat or flaunt herself to others —women or men.

But the weird thing was, Griff's awkward advance—awkward on her behalf, not his—had caused some sudden sensual stirrings that she'd not felt in a very long time. It wasn't the same with Marilyn. When they were together, her sensuality was on fire, raw, electric, and taboo.

What she'd felt with Griff—those subtle tingles of desire edged with an urge for more—reminded her of when she and George had just started dating.

Marilyn's arrival hadn't helped ease her anxiety, either. It only ramped it up. Normally, Alice was on top of things, but right now, she was at loose ends, dangling.

What the ever-loving hell? She wasn't attracted to men anymore. Right? What was this? Some sort of latent sexual identity confusion? Apparently, she was not as well-adjusted in the sexuality department as she'd once thought.

Beach week can't come soon enough.

She needed girlfriend time. Beach therapy. Maybe it was hormonal. *Good grief, am I in menopause? Or what do they call it— perimenopause? Is this a midlife crisis?*

Get a grip, Alice. You're losing it.

"Alice? Alice! Come join us back here."

Jerking herself from her musing, she spotted Marilyn waving from the back. Matt waved too before he ducked out the back door, leaving again.

With a sigh, Alice headed toward the war room.

"MATT ASKED TO TAKE NEXT WEEK OFF. IT'S HIS FAMILY reunion in Tennessee, and his mother is insisting he go. He's still basically a kid, so I told him it was fine."

Alice stared across the table at Marilyn. With two weeks to go before the debate, they had a major event to pull off and debate prep work to do. Next week was not a good time for Matt to be gone—they were short-staffed that week, anyway.

"But next Tuesday is Charlotte—the Mecklenburg County Democratic Party fundraiser. Remember?"

"Of course, I remember."

"Plus, we need to spend time on the debate." They'd worked on scripting potential questions and responses, had watched footage of Faust's past interviews, speeches, and impromptu conversations caught on film, but very soon they needed to actually practice. "I was hoping you and Matt could hold some mock debate sessions later next week after Charlotte."

"It will be fine. I've already told him he could go."

Alice eyed her. "I wish you had discussed that with me, Marilyn. I *am* his supervisor."

Her gaze darted back. "And I'm *your* supervisor, so I decided. Besides, we were on the road, and he needed an answer. I got Jonathan to agree."

Jonathan? That was confusing. "What does Jonathan have to do with this?"

Marilyn fully faced her. "Alice. Think! If Matt isn't going to Charlotte, then you need to go. Find someone here in the office to take charge at the headquarters while you're away. We have a couple of competent workers out there, I know. Bring one of them up to speed."

Alice felt like she'd just been slapped in the face. "I can do that—

but I can't go to Charlotte. Perhaps with everything going on you've forgotten, but I've already scheduled that week off. It's beach week, and you know I don't miss beach week. Pretty sure Matt knew that too, which is probably why he went around me." *And why he ducked out again before I got back here.*

"Matt is a professional. He wouldn't do that. You can miss beach week this year. Charlotte is important."

And beach week is important. Especially now. Alice stood. "No. I'm not missing beach week. I need the time off, and I gave you plenty of notice weeks ago. You *know* how important this is to me."

Marilyn quit shuffling papers and slowly looked up. "This is not the time for you to go play in the sand, Alice. Or drink tequila sunrises. Or smoke weed all day. Whatever decadent stuff you girls do. I never understood it all, anyway."

That whole idea landed rather crosswise with Alice.

No, Marilyn would never understand because frankly, Marilyn didn't have girlfriends or long-term female relationships—except for her. A lover. Suddenly, she wondered how many other long-term female lovers she'd had over the years.

So, what was her usual M.O. in these kinds of situations with Marilyn? Offer a solution she couldn't refuse.

"Look. We have a few days. Matt and I will get someone else prepped to travel with you. I have someone in mind. She's in her mid-thirties and has political experience. Very polished and eager to work for you. She was a White House intern during Obama's second term. She'll be great."

Marilyn shook her head. "No. I need *you* with me in Charlotte." She turned her attention to her laptop, scrolling through a website. "Faust is planning to be in Raleigh the same day. We have to make sure he doesn't upstage us."

She's totally dismissing me.

For a moment, Alice was unsure of what to say or do next. That Marilyn—the woman she'd given up her marriage for, had uprooted her family for, had loved wholeheartedly for fourteen years—was totally disregarding her needs, her input, and her feelings? That was unacceptable and unfathomable.

And *that*, did not sit well with Alice, either. Not at all.

"I'm not going."

"Don't be ridiculous," Marilyn said, still looking at her laptop. "Is there any coffee around here?"

All Alice could do for a moment was stare at her. Marilyn wasn't budging.

Finally, she met Alice's gaze. "Coffee?"

"Right."

Without a word, Alice left the room, passing the coffee station without a glance.

How dare they? Both of them!

She didn't trust Matt right now, and was royally pissed at Marilyn. Why did she think she could treat her in that manner? Totally dismiss her, *then request fucking coffee?*

But isn't that how she'd always treated you?

She hustled to her desk, where she typed a quick email, pressed send, gathered her things in her overly large tote bag, and then left the headquarters.

To hell with it all. To hell with them.

Three blocks down the street, she knocked on Griff's coffee shop door.

Twelve

Alice waited for Griff to come downstairs and unlock the door. She knew he was on his way because she saw a light come on in an upstairs window, then in the hallway at the rear of the shop. The light filtered through the blinds on the door window. She also heard him yell down the stairs, "Coming!"

As he twisted the lock from the other side, peeking through the blinds, he smiled, and Alice wondered if she'd made a mistake.

Oh shit, this is a huge mistake.

Then the door swung open. Griff peeked around her to the dark street. "Is it raining?"

Alice blinked. "Excuse me?"

"Cashing in your rain check?"

"Oh." Alice blindly pushed past him and into the coffee shop. "I heard you had wine."

"Are you sure you wouldn't rather have a mocha?"

"Wine is good." She glanced around the dim-lit shop. Where would a bottle of wine hide itself in here? "I need to get away from the campaign for a while."

Griff closed and locked the door, then slowly rotated to face her. "Rough day?"

"You could say."

"One that calls for wine, I gather?"

She nodded, staring into his eyes. "And talk, my friend, if you are up to it."

He grinned then. "I'm up for talk."

She tossed him another glance. "So where do you hide the wine in this place?"

Griff took a step forward. "Upstairs."

"Ah." She held his gaze. Now or never, Alice. You came here to assert some independence. Do the unexpected. Well, here's unconventionality served up on a platter. "Lead the way."

She followed him up the back stairway to his apartment. He suggested she find a seat on the sofa while he fetched the wine. Alice settled into the corner of his brown leather sofa and leaned into the soft, oversized cushions.

After a moment, she exhaled and let her head fall back against the pillow.

"Wine for the lady," Griff said.

She opened her eyes and looked up at him—gray hair, shaggy beard, and those interesting blue-gray eyes. He was a good friend. And maybe that's all she needed tonight.

Except, honestly, she wanted more.

She wanted to feel wanted—and if she were getting the signals right, Griff might actually want her.

"Thank you." She took the glass of rose-colored wine and took a sip. "Nice."

"It is, isn't it? It's from Portugal."

"I'm not that into wine. So, wine grows in Portugal?"

Griff laughed. "Wine doesn't, but grapes do."

How stupid, Alice! "Of course." She took another sip. "Just testing you. I like this. It's light and kind of fruity."

"It does have notes of berries with floral hints."

"Um, whatever. I just know I like it."

They chatted for a while about different wines, her lack of winery knowledge, and his expertise. Griff kept her glass full, and the more he poured, the more relaxed she became.

The wine was splendid, actually. Sweet. And she liked sweet things, so she truly enjoyed it. And after nearly a bottle, her tongue felt a lot looser than earlier.

"Griff, I want to tell you something, but it's for your ears only, and you have to promise not to tell the gossip people who told you that George and I are separated, and that I am getting a divorce."

He laughed out loud. "Now, that was a mouthful."

"I think I don't know how to punctuate sentences in my brain when it's full of wine."

"No matter. I'm pretty sure I understood. So, what did you want to tell me?"

She lay back against the comfortable pillows. *I could get lost in here.* "Well, two things, actually. One is that I want to have sex with you tonight. That's why I came."

Both of Griff's eyebrows shot up.

"Too much? Too bold?"

"Not necessarily."

"Think I got you on that one."

"Shocked, actually, but I'm not appalled. Go on?"

Alice paused, then nodded. "Yes. The other thing is, you need to know that I'm gay."

His expression was unmoving for a few seconds. "Alright. And...?"

"Maybe I'm a lesbian," she added. "I'm not sure. And maybe I'm bisexual, which is probably more accurate. But the thing is, those gossip people in town? They were right. George and I are getting a divorce because I've been having an affair. With a woman."

He leaned a little closer. "Anyone I know?"

Alice took another sip of her wine. "Yes."

"Are you going to tell me?"

"No."

He grinned again. "I didn't think you would."

"Do you still want to have sex with me?"

Griff pulled back, cocking his head to the side, then reached for the wine. Grasping her glass, he refilled it. "Actually, Alice, I didn't say I wanted to have sex with you. You said you wanted to have sex with me, and—"

She interrupted. "You were sending all the signals earlier in the day."

He met her gaze full-on. "Really? I was sending sex signals? Honestly, Alice, I just want to get to know you better on a personal level. Sex? Perhaps I had hoped eventually, but no... That wasn't my intent this morning."

"But—"

"But since you've started this, I will ask you the same question—do you still want to have sex with me?"

She sighed, deep. "Yes. I do."

"Why?"

Pausing for a beat, searching his eyes, she thought about that. *Why do I want to have sex with Griff?* Ah, yes. "Because for once, and maybe just for tonight, I want to do whatever I damn well please, whatever I feel like doing. I've always catered to everyone else's needs. I've been the good girl, the mother hen, the fixer. Frankly, I'm tired of being reliable and predictable. And tonight, for once, I don't want to consider anyone else's needs but my own. Can you handle that?"

Griff studied her for a moment, then took her glass and set it on the coffee table. Rising, he grabbed her hand and steadied her on her feet. "Works for me."

EARLY THE NEXT MORNING, ALICE ROLLED OVER IN BED and looked into Griff's eyes. Those mesmerizing eyes were wide open and staring back. If only she could see them clearly through the haze in her head.

"Oh, hell," she whispered, rubbing her temple. Turning away, she dragged the sheet with her as she stood up. Unfortunately, one corner was still folded into the bed—or perhaps lodged under Griff, and he wasn't budging. She faced him again, tucking the fabric under her arms as best she could. "I'm sorry. That wine."

My head is pounding.

He chuckled. "Nothing to be sorry about, Alice." Then, stretching his arm toward her, he added, "Come back here."

The clock right behind his head told her the time was four-forty-five. Damn early, even for her. He must have noticed her looking.

"The alarm goes off at five. I need to be downstairs by five-thirty to get the coffee machines up and going. The bakery truck arrives at six."

"And you open at seven."

He leaned closer, the sheet slipping a little. "Correct. That means we have a few minutes to bang out a fast one before the alarm goes off."

Bang out a fast one. Ugh. Wrong.

Alice grimaced and rubbed her temple. She'd been a lot of things last night—seductress, aggressor, willing and eager participant, naughty temptress—but this morning, she wasn't entirely feeling the need for a predawn quickie.

She jerked the sheet. It came away from his body, and she stumbled backward. Noticing her pants slung over the foot of the bed, she snagged them. "Not really up for a bump-and-run, Griff. I need to get going."

"Right. Duty calls."

"Just need to get home and shower. Clear my head." *Of more than just the wine haze.*

"Work never ceases for you, does it?"

Work. Right. For the first time in decades, she had no work, no job—and that felt completely disorienting. Even more so than having sex with a man again.

Which was completely befuddling.

Balancing first on one foot, then the other, she stepped into her pants. Afterward, she spotted her panties on a chair, snatched them up, and stuffed them into her pocket. She dropped the sheet, slipped into her light sweater, and looked about again for her shoes.

"Out by the sofa."

"Right." *No clue where my bra is. Forget it.* Facing him then, she added, "Griff, the wine was lovely, and thank you for the conversation, and..." *Geez. What?* "Whatever that was we had last night. I apologize for being a little over the top. I hope you understand. It was a ridiculous day, and I...."

He got up and walked toward her, naked as a jaybird.

She tried not to go stiff as he wrapped his arms around her. She also tried not to press against his...parts, but was pretty sure she had failed.

"It's all good, Alice. Friends."

Pulling back, she met his gaze again. "Of course. Friends."

But when she turned and left, grabbing up her shoes and her bag in the other room, and hurriedly skipping down the staircase, she figured she had to find a new coffee shop, and soon, because friends don't fuck, and remain friends.

It changes everything.

And last night had definitely turned the tide for her. She just needed to figure out how.

SHE'D LEFT HER CAR ON THE STREET IN FRONT OF THE campaign headquarters. Fortunately, it was still dark outside, and few people were moving about. She saw only one set of headlights down the street. Hustling to her car, she got in, locked the door, and took a deep breath.

Then exhaled. Long. As if she were trying to rid herself of the essence of Griff.

Hell, he was probably all over her.

Did she smell like sex? Him?

I need a shower.

I need to talk to the girls.

Grabbing her phone from her bag, she located their group text—and even though it was five o'clock in the morning, sounded the alarm.

Alice: *9-1-1. Lunch. Sandcastle. Please.*

No one responded. Of course. It's five a.m. They were all asleep.

Alice: *Lia. Get us a table? Lunch is on me.*

Finally, little dots started jumping on her phone.

Julia: *I can make it. Are you okay?*

Alice: *No. Yes. Maybe. I did something.*

Maggie: *I'm in. What did you do?*
Alice: *Later. Not on phone.*
Julia: *But you are okay.*
Am I? Am I okay?
Alice: *I am. Will be. Just need you guys.*
Lia: *I'm up. I'll get a table. Noon?*
Alice: *Perfect. See you then.*

With a sigh, she started the car and pulled onto the street. Mindlessly, she drove the few blocks, turned toward the sound, and made her way into her subdivision—the older section of Tuckaway Bay.

Another turn and she was on her street, anticipating a long, hot shower—until she pulled into her driveway and saw George's SUV parked at the side of the house.

"Fuck. Me."

This, she did not need. Not today. Not right now.

Thirteen

Five-o-two. Five-o-three. Five-o-four.

George lay on his side, watching the numbers of the old digital clock on the nightstand roll over. Repeatedly. Consistently. He'd been awake since four-thirty-two, thinking about Alice, wondering where in the hell she was, and why he even cared. At this point, what did it matter? They'd been apart all summer, and neither of them had kept tabs on the other. Besides, she didn't know he was coming back today, so why stay home if she didn't want to?

He wondered how her summer had gone. Had she and Marilyn made any major decisions while he'd been away?

The front door latch clicked, drawing his attention to the sound. He lay still, listening, semi-relieved to have something else to focus on but the clock. Certainly, she'd noticed his vehicle in the side drive. Hadn't she? He supposed he'd find out soon enough.

She slipped up the stairs and quietly hustled by their bedroom. He heard the soft closing of the bathroom door. The house had only one full bath, with a tiny powder room downstairs off the kitchen. He waited a few seconds and then heard the shower, smelled the steam.

The door must have popped open a little, a quirk of the old

house. After a moment, he let his mind drift to the day he found out
Alice was cheating on him....

———

FIVE YEARS EARLIER....

THE TEACHER IN-SERVICE DAY WENT LONGER THAN HE
would have liked. While George understood the value of professional
development for his educational career, and he'd benefited from the
workshops, it was summer, and he didn't enjoy being away from his
family in the evenings.

"Definitely looking forward to family time this entire weekend,"
he muttered to himself as he pulled into the driveway.

Alice sat on the porch steps as he approached. He smiled, thinking
about the long weekend ahead. Shoving the car into park, he left his
curriculum notebook behind and headed for the house. Alice stood as
he approached, a half-smile on her face.

He ignored that. Or tried to. Was something wrong?

Quickly, he caught her up in his arms. She gave him a weak hug
and took a few steps backward.

She stood a few inches shorter than him, her gaze tilted up to
meet his.

"Where's Ella?" He looked behind her. "Inside?"

"She's at the movies with Marci, then spending the night with
her."

"Marci's parents are at the movie, right?"

"No, George. She's fine."

This was unusual. Wasn't it? "Oh? We're letting her go out unsu-
pervised with friends now?"

"She's almost fifteen. She's old enough."

He wasn't entirely sure he agreed. "I was just hoping to see her
tonight, so we could plan some things for the weekend."

"Tomorrow."

They stood in front of the house, looking at each other, and suddenly, George was worried. "Alice?"

She reached for his hand. "We need to talk. Come inside."

The tone of her voice was almost a warning, and he abruptly knew that somehow, things were going to change. He'd been concerned for a while that something was going on with Alice. His first reaction was to bombard her with questions, but alternately he let her take the lead.

She led him into the kitchen, went to the refrigerator, and handed him a beer. "Here. Sit down. Drink this."

"What in the world?" He took the beer.

"I need to tell you something, and you are going to be upset."

Shit. "Alice, tell me. Are you sick? Is it Ella?" Oh hell, he was going to lose one of them. Panic struck his chest, and he plopped down hard on a bar stool at the kitchen island. "Just tell me."

Alice took a deep breath and held his gaze. "George, I love you. I will always love you. You have been a part of my life for a very long time, and you will always have a piece of my heart."

"But." He stood and shoved the beer aside. "There is a but coming with this speech, right?"

And he definitely hadn't expected that.

"But I'm not *in love* with you any longer."

He rarely got mad. And he wasn't angry right now, as much as he was hurt and confused—but suddenly, he wanted to crash his fist through something.

Alice met his gaze. "Talk, please."

"No, you. I think you have more to say. Go on."

Alice slowly nodded. "I am in love with someone else."

His head spun, crazy circles in his brain, and he sat again. In a flash, his entire life, or what he knew of his life, was spiraling out of control, images flashing in his head, his consciousness having difficulty keeping up with the commotion. "No."

Alice moved closer and sat beside him. "It's not what you think."

"Who is he?" He faced her. When she told him who the bastard was, he wanted her to look him in the eye.

"George." She said his name softly, almost pleading.

What did she want with him at this point? Why plead about anything?

"Tell me, Alice. How long has this been going on?"

She sighed. "George. Listen to me. I know you are upset, and this is a shock, but there is more I need to say. Please hear me out."

He wasn't sure he could even take in more information. "Whatever."

"I don't want a divorce. Not yet. I want us to wait for that. We can live here together, for Ella, amicably, until she gets out of school. I can do that. Can you?"

He stared straight at her. "While you're off fucking another man on the side? Are you insane?"

She shook her head. "No, George. There isn't a man."

He didn't understand. "What?"

"All these years, I didn't really know. But I can't keep it from you any longer. I'm gay."

"Excuse me?"

"I'm in love with a woman, George. And I have been for many years. But now it's time for you to know so we can make some plans—for Ella's future, and for our individual futures."

And there it was, even in a crisis, his Alice. Making sure everyone was alright. Seeing that everything was okay. Fixing things. Trying to, somehow, make it right.

Even when their world was falling apart.

Alice was gay? *What the ever-loving fuck?*

A FEW MINUTES AFTER ALICE'S SHOWER HAD FINALLY stopped, George sat up and pulled a pair of sweatpants on over his boxers. When she walked into the room in her bathroom, rubbing her wet hair with a towel, he looked up and into her eyes for the first time in eight weeks.

Her gaze skittered off.

"Alice." He nodded her way.

"I see you are home."

He reached for his T-shirt on a chair by the window. "We got in last night."

"Ella, too?"

"Of course. She wanted next week to get ready for school."

She tilted her head, thinking perhaps. "I see. I'm glad I'll get a little time with her." She paused momentarily, glancing about the room. "You slept in my bed. Why didn't you sleep in the spare room like you'd been doing?"

Her chin jutted up. In defiance, he supposed. Unlike her. Alice had rarely challenged him during their marriage, and vice versa. They were the easy-going, get-along couple.

He took a few steps closer. "You know, Alice? You don't get to make all of my decisions, including which bed I sleep in."

"But that's my bed."

He turned and pointed. "No, that's our bed. It's been our bed for over twenty years and, dammit, when I came home last night, I wanted to sleep in it. Not in some cold, impersonal guest room with ruffled pillow shams and doilies on the dresser. I wanted *my* bed." Pausing, he angled himself and took another step so that he could see her eyes. "And I had hoped *my wife* would be in it with me."

Her eyes widened. "You know that's not happening."

"Alice, look. We need to talk. I've been doing a lot of thinking—"

"No, George. Stop."

She waved her hands, as if warning him away from that discussion. He could sense something—insecurity?—in her actions. Perhaps there was hope?

"Why didn't you tell me you were coming? We can't be here together. We have to live apart for several more months."

Well, hello to you too, sweetheart. He wondered when she'd get to that. Didn't take long.

"Calm down, Alice. I've put out a few feelers for apartments, but nothing has materialized. Something will come up." That was a true statement—sort of. He'd made some calls. Looked at some places online. But nothing appealed to him, even though there were available options.

"But this screws with the plan. You did this on purpose."

"I did no such thing. Goodness, get a grip. You weren't even here, so why does it matter? I'm assuming you spent the night with Marilyn."

The look on her face was a bit perplexing, neither a guilty expression nor a startled one. Just deadpan, frozen, as if... As if she were hiding something.

Interesting.

"Don't make assumptions." She turned and headed for the closet, which doubled as her dressing room, tossing the damp towel into the hamper on her way.

He took a few steps and slanted his gaze inside, watching her pull down a summer sundress and hook its hanger over the door frame. Moving to her lingerie chest, she stared into the mirror on top, fluffing her damp hair, then attacked the tangles with a comb.

George stepped up behind her and gauged her worried expression in the reflection.

She briefly eyed him back, then glanced off. "What?"

"You weren't with Marilyn?"

"I don't have to answer to you, George."

"That's right. You don't."

She jerked the comb through her hair. He remembered a time when they were a lot younger, and when her hair was longer, that she'd asked him to comb her hair out. He'd offer again, but knew he'd get shot down, so he wasn't about to extend that invitation.

She was angry at finding him there, obviously, and in their bed—but there was something else lurking behind that anger. What? He hadn't a clue.

"I still wish I knew you were coming. If the subject ever comes up, like with our lawyers or anything, we did not stay under the same roof."

"And that would not be a lie."

"Right."

Of course, he wasn't concerned. Did he care if they had to start the year over? No. He was absolutely fine with that. Because being gone had done him a world of good. He'd had more than ample time to think about their situation and consider alternatives.

And he'd decided. He wanted his life back.

He wanted *his wife* back.

Alice dropped her robe and stood with her back to him, naked. She rifled through the dresser drawer for panties and a bra. He watched her slip into both, as he'd done thousands of times during their years together, but for the first time in a very long time, his breath caught in his throat. His gaze traveled her body, from her slim neck and narrow shoulders to her curvy backside. He loved the sweep of her back, the round arch of her bottom, the subtle dip in her spine.

This time was different. Watching her wasn't a daily, mundane thing. This was something he'd not experienced much in years. He'd missed her body—seeing it, touching it, lying next to it—and he'd missed the simple act of watching her get dressed in the morning.

She turned slightly, reaching for the dress in the doorway, and slid him a brief glance. Almost seductive. A fleeting, alluring look.

Did she realize what she was doing?

Sexual awareness shot through him, and he could barely contain it. God, he wanted her, right then. Right now. It had been too long, dammit. Quickly, he stepped back into the bedroom—mostly because he didn't want her to see him getting hard, or for Alice to suspect that her nakedness was turning him on.

But why shouldn't she expect that?

Leave her alone, George. Give her space. Take your time.

She breezed into the bedroom carrying a pair of sandals and broke his mood. He tried to make eye contact. "I always liked that dress." It was a simple, sleeveless summer dress, one she'd often worn when sunning herself on the dock, or out for an afternoon of shopping on a hot summer day.

"Thanks." She slipped one foot, then the other, into her strappy sandals.

"Casual Tuesday at work?"

She didn't miss a beat. "Not working today."

"Oh?"

"No. I'm off."

"Good." He paused. "Alice, I want to talk about our marriage. About everything. I think we're making a mistake."

Alice righted herself, then finally met his gaze directly, peering into his eyes. "I'm going to the resort. The girls are waiting for me. Sorry."

He glanced again at the clock. Was it that easy for her to dismiss him? "It's not even six yet. Pretty sure most of your friends aren't even up."

She broke the connection between them and headed for the door. "It's a day thing, starting with breakfast."

"Can't you give me fifteen minutes this morning?"

She hesitated at the door, then angled back and met his gaze. "George," she began softly. "Please don't make this any harder than it already is."

"It doesn't have to be difficult. If it is hard, then maybe we're doing the wrong thing."

She shook her head. "I have to go. The girls...."

"But you will see them next week. You have beach week, right?"

She turned. "So?"

He gave up. *Whatever.* "Fine. Have fun. Ella and I will see you later this evening. Shall I cook?"

She stared again. "Sure. Give her my love."

"I'm sure she would rather hear that from you."

But she ignored him rather than responding and left.

Fourteen

Alice pulled into the beach access lot close to Quigley Pier. She sat for quite a while, letting her mind settle, while looking up at the sandy dune, the steps leading over it, and the pale blue summer sky beyond. The ocean and pier were just on the other side. While she preferred her dock on the sound, rather than the wind and sand of the ocean shoreline, this was nice, too. She'd not walked the beach in the early morning for a long time. Maybe she'd find a shell or two for keeping. Even luckier, a piece of elusive sea glass, an uncommon find on the Tuckaway Bay beaches.

More than anything, she needed to be alone.

Leaving her car, she climbed the stairs and headed for the pier. Quigley's was a local landmark. The Quigley family was said to be among the early settlers, making their business originally in trade, and then in later years, fishing and seafood restaurants. About seventy-five years ago, they built the pier on oceanfront property the family had owned for generations. Locals gathered at the pier house for bait and tackle, coffee, and bullshit, and at the day's end, a beer or two. There was no charge to fish on the pier if you were a Tuckaway Bay resident, but vacationers had to pay a hefty fee—which kept most of them away, since other piers charged much less.

The point, Alice was certain.

The place was nothing fancy, full of local color, and one of her favorite spots when she wanted to be alone.

Alice took the steps to the landing, then the walkway around the bait and tackle shop, and headed for the far end of the pier, projecting out over the Atlantic. The sun was up now, and she was sad she'd missed the sunrise. But what she needed more than a sunrise was quiet reflection.

And space to clear her head.

What the hell had she done last night?

On the one hand, she felt remorse and probably some guilt. On the other, she felt emboldened with a type of power she wasn't sure she'd ever before felt.

Remorse, because it felt like she'd used Griff, and she worried she'd damaged their friendship.

Guilt because... Well, Marilyn. They were supposed to be a couple. Right? But honestly, they've never been a true couple. So why?

Then there was George. She'd not expected to see him immediately after leaving Griff's bed. The guilt when she saw him hit her full force and was unexpected.

She had to push all that away. She was her own woman. She made her own decisions. And that's where the powerful part came in.

She had decided. Hadn't she?

She'd owned it. And she'd own the consequences, too.

Just like she'd owned the consequences all those years ago, when Marilyn had set out to seduce her, claim her—and Alice had finally given in.

YEARS EARLIER....

ALICE CLOSED HER EYES AGAINST THE LATE AFTERNOON glare pouring into her office space. Pinching the bridge of her nose was not the best way to get rid of an approaching migraine, she knew, but pinch she did as she squinted over listing copy and sales data.

She needed caffeine. Hadn't left her desk all day though. And wouldn't.

Shit. She might avoid the kitchen and the coffeemaker and Marilyn, but she couldn't avoid the restroom for much longer.

She hadn't slept for two nights. All she could think of was how Marilyn had made her feel—alive, excited, energized, and then rejected and embarrassed—as she'd left her, wanting more.

But that was her M.O. perhaps. Leaving her wanting?

Fool. What a fool I am.

Before I invest myself, I want you to be certain.

Certain about what? That she liked women better than men? That she wanted to make some sort of commitment to Marilyn? Why would she do that? She was married, for God's sake. They both were.

Deeper. Maybe it goes much deeper.

What the hell was she talking about? Deeper?

Emotion? Feelings? Caring for someone.

Well, that was just too damned bad. She didn't want to let her feelings go too deep. She couldn't. She had George and Ella. *They* deserved her deep feelings and emotions—not Marilyn.

So, it is about sex then? Is it that shallow?

"Alice?"

Her head jerked up, but she said nothing.

Marilyn stared. "Well?"

"Well, what?"

"How are you?"

How am I? "What do you *want*?"

Marilyn pulled an office chair closer to her desk and sat. "Oh, sweet Alice, you're angry and hurt." She crossed her legs and leaned back in the chair, folding her arms over her chest. Alice's gaze was drawn to her legs—long, shapely, sheathed in silk stockings, pleated together like the pages of a book.

Alice closed her eyes against the scene. *Angry and hurt.* "Not angry," she said.

"Hurt, then."

"Puzzled, perhaps."

"Oh, my sweet," Marilyn cooed, leaning forward. "I know that was difficult for you but very necessary."

She'd about had enough. "Marilyn, I'm not interested in playing games. What is it you want from me? Because I'm uncertain."

"I want you, Alice," she said calmly.

Me? "You want me."

"Yes."

"Hell of a way to show it, walking out."

Placing her manicured fingers on the desktop, Marilyn edged closer. "I thought I had made it perfectly clear why I left. And if you think that was easy, it was not."

Before I invest myself, I want you to be certain.

Alice chuckled. "Yes, and I want to be certain myself. Isn't that the way it is with relationships, Marilyn? We all want to be certain. Thing is, certainty is never a sure thing with couples, is it? Especially when dabbling on the side."

"It can be."

"Not in my experience." She shoved a few things into her purse. Keys. Cell phone. The damned day planner.

"Then maybe you've had the wrong kinds of experiences."

She tugged her bag over her shoulder and took a step toward the door. "And you're my right experience?"

She paused, watching her. "Alice, I'll be blunt. We can live in two worlds. All we need to do is create the mindset that allows it. We can have our world with our husbands and families. And we can have a world together, just us, too. Keeping them separate is the key."

Alice paused, her hand on the doorknob, and her back to Marilyn. "Impossible," she said.

"It's not."

Turning, she met Marilyn's gaze. "How so?"

"All you have to do is allow it to happen, Alice. It all depends on you."

Me? Why the fuck is it up to me?

She didn't hesitate. "Well, if that's the case, don't hold your breath."

SLEEP WAS THE ONE THING SHE NEEDED AND THE LAST thing coming to her. The conversation she'd had with Marilyn late that afternoon, when she'd thrown all the decision making on Alice, sat uncomfortably on her brain.

She had no clue how to handle the situation.

Alice contemplated bourbon and decided against it. Even though George was still at the teacher's conference, and Ella was spending the night with a friend, she didn't want to wake up hungover. Besides, she had a lot of work to finish in the morning.

A steamy shower didn't help, either. It only conjured up images of her and Marilyn washing each other's hair, shampoo bubbles sliding over their bodies. Of their hipbones touching in gentle persuasion and their hands exploring flesh and forbidden crevices.

Wrapping the kimono around herself after drying off, she released her hair from the clip holding it up. Peering into the mirror, she fluffed the length and picked at a few damp tendrils about her face. Pausing, she peered deep into her eyes, searching for...something.

Truth?

Admittance? Wonder?

Acceptance?

Sooner or later, I'll get frustrated and find other prey.

And that was the last thing she wanted.

Panic gripped her chest, and suddenly, she realized—she didn't want Marilyn to find other prey. She wanted to *be* Marilyn's prey.

Racing toward the nightstand, she snatched up her cell phone and scrolled for Marilyn's number. Even though she had never called her, she had all the office staff stored in her contacts. Work purposes. She found her name and punched the key.

Please.

Please.

Ringing. Ringing. Voice mail.

Dammit.

"Marilyn. Marilyn, it's Alice. Look, can we talk? I need to talk. Please call."

She gripped the phone tightly, not entirely willing to turn the thing off, to break the one connection she had with her at the moment.

Too late?

What if I am too late?

She wandered downstairs and sat on the living room sofa, folding her arms around her as though she were containing the gnawing ache she felt inside.

Too. Damned. Deep. Inside.

A soft, hesitant knock sounded at the door.

Alice sat up straighter, listening. It didn't come again.

Don't let her get away.

Alice rushed through the entryway and opened the door.

Marilyn.

Alice unlatched the screen door and nudged it open. Without words, Marilyn crossed the threshold. Closer now, she took Alice into her arms.

The prey is caught.

Pulling away from her warmth, Alice grasped Marilyn's hand and led her upstairs to the bedroom. Her kimono fell to the floor in a fluid puddle.

Fifteen

At Quigley Pier, Alice watched the dolphins dance on the waves, and the pelicans and seagulls scope the ripples for food. She'd stayed there, at the far end of the wharf, for a good hour or longer. The few fishermen ignored her, and she them, although she heard their shouts from time to time as they reeled in a fish.

Recalling her first sexual encounters with Marilyn had opened her eyes. Even though she and George had been married for years, she was still very innocent, sexually. Over time, Marilyn had introduced her to a whole new world of pleasurable experiences, and before long, she'd been hooked. Unable to let it go. And Marilyn?

Marilyn knew exactly what she was doing.

Prey was right. Oh, she might have loved Alice, but she also enjoyed the conquest just as much—and maybe more. The night she'd left her unsatisfied, and wanting, solidified her intent. And now, years later, Alice wondered how she'd let herself get caught up in it all.

She'd been needy, she supposed, in some ways.

The experience with Griff was similar.

But there was one big difference between Marilyn and Griff. Marilyn had pursued and seduced Alice. With Griff, the tables were turned. She'd been the pursuer, although Griff didn't require much seduction.

None of it was okay—but she was human, and no human was perfect. Not even her.

She'd cheated on George with Marilyn. And now she'd cheated on George *and* Marilyn, with Griff.

Going after what she wanted, rather than waiting for Marilyn to dribble out her crumbs of affection, was powerful. And she'd be damned if she'd let morning-after remorse get the best of her.

After a while, her phone buzzed in her bag, and Alice reached for it.

Lia: *I reserved a table for eleven. Too early?*
Alice: *Not for me.*
Julia: *See you then.*
Maggie: *Good for me too.*
Alice: *I'm at Quigley's. I'll take a stroll that way in a bit.*
A few seconds ticked by.
Lia: *You ok?*
Alice: *Yeah. See you soon.*

At about nine-thirty, she ambled toward the Sea Glass Inn, stopping occasionally to inspect a shell or other sea find. Her mind wandered as she moseyed along, sometimes thinking, and sometimes just letting the breeze and the water's edge clear the cobwebs.

The hotel came into view about an hour later.

Five clam shells, two chipped scallops, a scotch bonnet, a few pretty pebbles, and a medium-sized whelk rounded out her collection. A good day. Her sundress pockets were heavy as she entered the Sandcastle, and she wondered if she should have stashed her treasures somewhere outside.

Maybe.

She started to turn back when Belle, Lia's daughter, waved her over to a table—so she and her heavy pockets headed that way.

She kissed Belle's cheek. "It's been too long. How is baby Grace?"

"Chubby and demanding." Belle laughed. "She's great, actually. Most of the time she comes to work with me in the office, but today they needed some extra help here. I have a sitter for days like this."

"That's good." Alice sat while Belle placed menus at each seat. "I'm early."

"It's fine. Coffee?"

"Too early for a margarita?"

Belle smiled. "Never. Coming right up." She headed toward the bar where her stepfather, Zach, was playing bartender.

Alice turned her focus out the window, watching sunbathers gather at the pool. Beyond that, she could see clumps of vacationers claiming their beach spots for the day with umbrellas and beach chairs and coolers. One group worked to set up a volleyball net. To the right, near the edge of the resort property, she could see the Gull Cottage, where Maggie was staying this summer with her kids, and a couple of fishermen casting into the ocean.

After a few minutes, she heard a familiar voice.

"I thought I would beat you here. But no...."

"Maggie." With a quick swivel, she stood and gave her friend a hug. "You look great."

"I'm rested, and that's a good thing." She sat catty-corner from Alice. "I'm worried about you, though."

She shrugged. "Just another day in paradise."

"Can paradise handle two more?"

Julia and Lia also approached the table. Alice glanced at her watch. "It's early. Why are you all here now?"

The two settled in their chairs, and then Lia looked directly at Alice. "We're here because you are. Belle texted that you were early." Lia stretched her hand across the table and touched Alice's fingertips. "Plus, you were at Quigley's, your go-to spot when you're upset. We're worried about you."

"I'm okay."

"Really?" Julia asked.

"Yes. I had a thought-provoking conversation with a dolphin, and a long meandering beach walk. So, I'm good. Better anyway."

"Really?" Julia asked again.

"No. Not really. But I will be fine."

Maggie leaned toward her. "We're all here to help. What can we do?"

Alice exhaled. "Maybe just listen?"

Belle interrupted, setting the margarita in front of Alice. "Here you go."

"Oh, thank you." Even though the wine probably wasn't fully out of her system, she needed the tequila. Chalk it up to more new experiences.

Lia questioned, "Day drinking?"

"Why not?" Alice took a sip. "Join me? Well, not you, Julia."

Julia grimaced. "Not a problem. I'm here to take over the mother hen role since you are seemingly down for the count, and that requires sobriety. Not that I'd risk that, anyway. What's going on, Alice? We know it's something."

She looked at Belle. "Bring them beverages of their choice, on me." Then to her friends she said, "Drinks first."

"Fine," Julia noted. "But you are procrastinating."

Belle had barely turned to leave when Zach stepped up to the table with a tray of margaritas. "This one's for Julia," he said, handing it to her. "Special order. And these are for the rest of you."

Lia beamed. "I've trained him well."

"They're on the house. I figured since Alice started the trend, the rest of you would follow her lead."

Maggie patted his arm. "You are a very good man, my friend. Now, be off with you. We have lady business to tend to."

Zach gave a quick salute. "Yes, ma'am. I imagine there is beach week planning and all that."

The women nodded, glancing at each other, faces expressionless, as if hiding a secret.

Zach left without another word.

They all stared at Alice.

She swallowed hard. "I quit the campaign. I have no job."

They kept staring. After a moment, Maggie said, "That's all? I thought this would be juicier news."

"Well," Lia said, "let's think about this for a minute. If you quit the campaign, does that mean something is going on between you and Marilyn?"

"Oh, right." Maggie leaned into the conversation then. "What caused you to quit? Did you two fight?"

"Partly." She paused, thinking. "No, more than partly. She told me I can't have next week off, that I needed to go to Charlotte with her for an event there. Matt has a family commitment."

"You quit because of beach week?" Julia tilted her head.

"No. I quit because she was devaluing me, not listening to me, and disregarding my input and my wishes. She ignored me and frankly, she was mean about it."

Lia drummed her fingers on the table. "You've mentioned that she has a teeny bit of a temper."

Julia agreed. "Yes, but I don't get quitting the campaign, Alice. You loved doing that work. Why would you deprive yourself of something you love doing because Marilyn is being a piss-pants?" She stared hard at Alice. "There's something you're not telling us."

Truth. Everything they said. All true.

"I quit because I don't feel seen. Not in the campaign. Not in the relationship. I'm easily dismissed and looked over—until someone needs something. And then? Well, good ol' Alice will get it done."

Julia sat back. "Alice...."

"I know, I know..." She lurched forward, slapping a hand on the table in front of Julia. "I know what you are about to say. I've played that role for years. I've intentionally made myself the fixer. I've put everyone else first. Why shouldn't people treat me that way, when I've allowed them? When I don't stand up for myself and my own needs?"

Maggie sighed. "Well, we really did appreciate it in college when you held our hair back as we puked and when you appointed yourself our designated driver every weekend."

"Maggie!" Julia frowned and scooted forward, her chair squeaking against the plank flooring. "Not the time."

Maggie stared. "Well, sure. But I meant that in a good way. We were appreciative. Weren't we?"

"And we didn't realize it back then, how much we were taking advantage of you," Lia said. "Expecting you to play that role. We're sorry."

Alice shook her head. "No, don't you see? That's the problem. It wasn't anything you all did. Oh, maybe you knew I would always be there, fix things, make sure you got home in one piece—but the problem was me. Me! I *wanted* to be the mother hen, because when I played that role, I knew I was needed."

Julia grasped her hand. "Oh, Alice."

Lia and Maggie said nothing more.

Alice leaned back in her seat. "So, I did something. For me."

"Good for you." Maggie reached for Alice's other hand.

"Right." Lia nodded.

Julia studied her. "What the fuck did you do?"

The woman can see through anything. Damn lawyer brain.

"Well, I went out and had sex."

Lia's jaw dropped.

"All right!" Maggie wiggled in her seat. "Details, please."

Julia shook her head. "I'm assuming this sexual encounter wasn't with Marilyn."

"No, it wasn't. I slept with Griff. The coffee shop guy."

To Alice, it felt like the entire room went soundless. Kind of like that spot in a horror movie where the music keeps getting louder, and the bass gets deeper, and the tempo escalates to a point where you almost can't stand it any longer, and then—

Silence.

Maggie squeezed her hand. "This is going to take more than one margarita."

"Definitely." Julia sat up straighter and motioned to Zach behind the bar. "Another round," she shouted. "And keep them coming, please."

He gave her a thumbs-up.

Lia looked at her with sympathy. "Do you feel guilty?"

Alice grinned. "No, I feel empowered. I set out to please myself, and I did it. I dealt with the guilt and remorse somewhat earlier on the pier—and I'll continue to work on that. But, the biggest thing I'm feeling right now is confusion. For most of my adult life, I've thought of sex in one way. And then came Marilyn, who introduced me to sex in a whole different way. And now? With Griff...?"

Maggie giggled. "Was it good?"

She laughed. "I was wine drunk and yes, it was damn good."

"Will you do it again?" Maggie prodded.

Alice thought about that for a moment. "I don't know. Maybe not with Griff." Her mind drifted back to her bedroom earlier, and George. "Something weird happened this morning."

Lia laughed. "Even weirder than what happened last night?"

"Yeah." Alice gave a slow nod. "George and Ella are back from the mountains. He was in our bedroom when I got home this morning. Apparently, he slept in my bed last night. I came home and showered. And then, I was naked in my dressing room while getting dressed, and suddenly, I got really turned on. I knew he was watching me, and I felt like a temptress. It was all I could do not to lure him to bed and jump his bones."

Lia's eyes grew big and round. "You didn't."

Maggie bounced in her seat. "You did. Didn't you?"

"Oh, shit." Julia drained her virgin margarita.

She paused, letting the idea of it all settle around them. "No, I didn't. But I half wanted to."

"Damn, Alice. Where have you been hiding your sexual self all these years?" Maggie fell back against her seat.

"Tucked neatly into my buttoned-up sexual straitjacket, I guess." She traced the stem of her margarita glass. *Have I even taken a sip?* "You know, before Griff, George was the only other man I'd ever slept with."

Lia blinked repeatedly. "Whoa."

"Seriously?" Julia asked.

"Oh, Alice, that is so sad." Maggie frowned. "This is something we need to definitely work through with you during beach week."

"Agreed." Lia bobbed her head.

Alice stared at the tabletop. "Perhaps. I feel like the door to my sexuality is opening wider. Who am I, really? Am I gay? Bi? A lesbian? Straight? Do I even have to choose a label, and why do I need one, anyway? Can't I just be me and make choices when they are presented to me?"

Maggie slapped her hand on the table. "You go, girl!"

"It might be time to explore my options."

Julia raised her glass. "No time like the present. You're at a cross-roads, Alice. If not now, when?"

Lia sipped her margarita, then sighed. "Well, all I can say is that it's been a year so far—babies, funerals, divorces, kids leaving the nest, AWOL friends—and I'm glad beach week is just around the corner." She tipped her glass to the crew. "We have a very full itinerary for beach therapy."

"That we do." Julia pushed her glass aside. "Before we dive deep into anything else, I do want to suggest something for next week, if I may."

"Does it have to do with me?" Alice asked.

"Or me?" Maggie arched a brow.

"It involves all of us," Julia explained. "I know beach week has been ours exclusively for over twenty years—but now we all have young women in our lives who are just getting to know each other. I value my friendship with all of you more than anything, and I wonder if our girls need a similar connection? Should we invite them to beach week for a day and night? The next generation. What do you think?"

"Oh, I don't know," Maggie said. "They certainly had their moments over Christmas. Do you think we are inviting disaster?"

"I thought about that," Julia said, "but I was hoping some time together would help them get over the stuff that happened then."

"Yeah, maybe," Maggie replied.

Alice wondered how Ella would react to the idea. "I love it, but... Is pushing our friendship off on the daughters wise? Shouldn't they find their own circles of friends, and not feel forced to create the same kind of bond we have?"

"That's a point," Maggie said, "but even if they don't connect like we did, they already have bonds through us. I think a day together with all the girls would be awesome, actually. For everyone."

"Agreed," Lia added. "Let them take it where they want to take it, then."

It might work. And Ella could possibly benefit. Alice nodded. "Alright. Ella leaves for school the Monday after beach week, and I would like to have a little more time with her. What day were you thinking?"

"What about Thursday?" Julia said. "They could come early in the day, we'd either cook in or go out to eat, then they could spend the night and leave the next morning. I'll just add that I do have an ulterior motive. Hannah is coming to see her dad next week anyway, and I really want some girl time with her."

Hannah. Alice actually wouldn't mind talking to her, since she works with young adults around LGBTQ+ issues. Alice wasn't a young person by any stretch, in physical age, but regarding her sexuality, she was barely a toddler. "Thursday works for Ella, I'm sure, but I'll ask."

Maggie leaned forward. "I'll check with Carol. She was going to watch Jason and Chloe, but maybe they can hang out with Zach that day?" She glanced at Lia.

"And Sam," Julia said.

"Right."

"Belle can get her sitter, and Grandpa Zach can be on duty at night. I think we're good then?"

They all nodded, glancing across the table at each other.

"Now we just need to get the girls to agree," Julia said.

"And get along," Lia added.

"Oh sure," Maggie uttered. "Piece of cake."

GEORGE PUSHED THE DOOR OPEN TO THE STREET AT THE bottom of the staircase. Ella followed him outside onto the sidewalk. The afternoon sun angled just so that it almost blinded him as he moved away from the dark hallway.

"Do you think that one will work, Dad?"

"Not a candidate."

"I didn't think so either."

They strolled down a side street off Main, heading toward the town center. "I wouldn't mind living downtown," he told her. "It's close enough to school, convenient to restaurants and shopping, but the Food Lion is a few miles further away."

"True. But it's not like you go there every day."

"Right."

He stopped, glancing back at the building, his gaze traveling up to the second floor. "But that apartment... Too dark, I think. Don't you? Even if I replaced those heavy curtains, it's just too...moody."

Ella gave him a crooked grin. "You're just used to how mom decorates—light and airy."

"I suppose you're right."

"You could always paint," she suggested.

"True."

"But you don't want to, do you?"

"I don't think it's the place for me. Let's keep looking."

Ella agreed. "Where's that newspaper?"

George pulled the folded classified section from his back pocket.

Ella snatched it and, with an eye roll, popped it open and scrolled the apartment listings again. Tuckaway Bay was small-town, and his daughter continually reminded him of how backward the town was.

"Who even reads newspapers anymore?" she muttered. "You know we could search online."

"True that."

"But you don't want to do that either. Do you?"

He stared across the street.

"Dad?"

His gaze was fixed on Marilyn's campaign headquarters. He could see people bustling about inside through the wide glass windows. But not Alice, not today. Where was she?

He wasn't buying the all-day girlfriend explanation. Was Marilyn on the road?

With a sigh, Ella tossed the newspaper into a nearby trash receptacle. "Dad? I'm serious. What do you want? Really?"

Oh, this girl. His heart ached for her, and for him. Their family. No one wanted what was happening in their lives right now.

Except for Alice.

"Sweetheart," he whispered, reaching for her hand. "What I want, I will not get."

"And why is that?"

"Oh, you know why."

Ella stepped closer and grasped his other hand. She stood before him looking up, and suddenly she was his little girl again, a decade ago. "Dad," she whispered. "Let's go home and make a family dinner. Let's fight to get Mom back."

Sixteen

They left the Sandcastle around four o'clock that afternoon. Lia headed upstairs to her apartment at the inn, and Maggie to the Gull. Julia drove Alice home, since her car was still parked at Quigley Pier. Walking back to the pier was out of the question—it was hot, and she was slightly buzzed.

As for driving home? Nope. Four margaritas.

Enough said.

Julia pulled to the curb in front of Alice's house about twenty minutes later. "If you want me to come back later tonight, or in the morning, to get your car, just let me know."

Alice nodded. "Thanks, Julia. I'm sure George or Ella can help me, but if not, I will definitely give you a shout." She leaned closer and gave her a hug, knowing that hugs were not Julia's thing. "Thank you," she whispered, "for the ride and for being my friend. And for not judging me."

When she pulled back, she noted Julia's warm smile, then left the car and headed for her front porch.

To be honest, she wasn't sure she was ready to face the evening with George and Ella and tamped down a few seconds of panic. But before she could put her hand on the screen door handle, Ella pushed through to the porch.

"Mom! I'm so glad you are home." She wrapped her arms around Alice and hugged her close. "I've missed you," she whispered.

Alice drew back, her eyes stinging. "Oh, sweetheart. I've missed you too. You were asleep when I came in last night."

"And gone again before I got up. It's okay. I'm glad we're having dinner together tonight." Ella linked her arm with hers and they headed inside.

"I can't believe it's time for you to go back to school."

"The summer flew."

"I want to spend as much time together as we can," Alice told her. She paused for a moment, thinking through her next words. "And the good news is, I'm not working now, so I have more time."

Ella looked sideways at her, slowing her steps. "You're not working for...her?"

Alice shook her head. "No. It's for the best."

It seemed a million questions flitted over Ella's face, but she said nothing.

"I haven't told your dad. Let's talk about that more later."

Ella gave a slight nod. "Sure, Mom."

Then Alice remembered the beach week idea. "But you know next week is beach week. Right?"

"I know, Mom. It's okay. We have almost ten days."

"Yes. But Julia had a great idea—we can discuss that more later, too—but would you want to come to beach week for a day and night? With the other girls? Hannah is flying in."

Ella halted and turned toward Alice. Her smile faded a little and quickly righted itself, then her words flowed as if she were afraid she couldn't get them all in. "Let's talk later, like you said. Dad's in the kitchen. He ordered a seafood boil, and they just delivered it. Oh, God, I'm so ready for seafood. We had nothing but steak and hamburgers in the mountains. And sandwiches. I'm making a salad, and we were wondering if you could make the lemonade? Yours is always the best. Would you?"

How could she refuse? Her daughter's facial expression had gone from confused to joyous in seconds. If fresh-squeezed lemonade would make her baby girl happy, then of course she would make lemonade. "Lead me to the lemons!"

They laughed and moved into the kitchen.

George looked up from where he was cleaning a few ears of sweet corn. He looked directly at her. "Well, hello. Have a good day?"

Honestly, that was not what she'd expected from him. Where's the interrogation? *Where have you been? Who were you with? What were you doing?*

"The day was good. Long." She sat on a barstool at the kitchen island and watched him work. "I had too many margaritas."

He raised an eyebrow and grinned. "Oh? How many?"

"Four, but spread out over five hours, so I'm pretty much un-buzzed by now. Maybe we can get my car later. Julia brought me home."

"Of course," he said. "Where is it?"

"Quigley Pier."

He studied her for a moment, then resumed picking silk from the corn. "I see. Hungry?"

No questions. No argument.

"Starving. The boil smells good."

"It won't be long. I thought we might need more corn than what they provided."

Ella stood by the refrigerator. "Mom, let's get your lemons."

"Oh, right."

She passed George. He looked up and grinned as she did. His smile was warm, caring, attentive. Like her old George. And it was....

Nice. It was nice.

Alice took the bag of lemons from Ella and set them on the island countertop next to George. "Great. Lemons and sugar and water. Maybe a sprig of mint. Ella, would you mind seeing if there is any out back that isn't wilted from all this heat?" She looked at her daughter and chuckled. "What was it you used to say? A sprigomint?"

Ella burst out laughing. "Oh my God, yes. I forgot about that. Sprigomint."

George laughed, too. "You always got words mixed up when you were little. You couldn't have been more than six when you said that." He tugged on Ella's arm then and pulled her into his side. Alice thought she saw a glint of moisture in his eyes. "I sure wish we had those days back again," he whispered, then looked at Alice. "They went by too fast."

She almost choked up. "Yes, they did." Snatching at the bag of lemons, she went to the sink and quickly swiped her eyes. "The mint, Ella?"

"Be right back."

Ella left out the back door. George looked over at her and they made eye contact again.

"Dinner smells good," she said quietly. "Thanks for doing that."

"I thought maybe it would be nice for all of us."

"You're always so thoughtful."

He stopped picking at the corn and faced her, peering deep into her eyes. "I want normal for once, Alice. Can we do that tonight? Even if it's just one more time?"

She had to fight her tears and gently nodded. "Yes. Normal would be nice. I would like that."

"Me, too." His smile broadened then—that lovely George smile she fell in love with back in high school. Just a few decades ago.

"Good. Then let's get dinner on the table."

<hr>

THREE HOURS LATER, THE DINNER DISHES CLEARED AND washed, and the kitchen tidied up, they sat around the table playing Monopoly. George was winning, of course. He always won. Even after all these years, Alice had never figured out his strategy.

Ella quickly bought up Park Place and Boardwalk, which was her tactic from the git-go. She enjoyed snagging those high-priced properties, buying hotels, and charging rent, then sitting back to hoard the rest of her money. Alice's usual M.O. was simply to buy up everything as it came to her—if she had the funds—with no plan of action.

It rarely worked.

She sighed and watched Ella and George rib each other and banter about. They were close. Always had been. Even if she were permanently out of the picture, they would always have each other. Could she say the same? Would Ella be there for her, just as she was for George?

Would that be difficult for Ella, dividing her loyalties between her parents?

But it doesn't have to be one or the other, Alice. There shouldn't be any taking of sides. What if there is a way to put this family back together again?

Her subconscious was working overtime.

Would she want that? To be back with George, and the three of them a family again?

"Mom, it's your turn."

She pulled out of her musing and tossed the dice and drew a card. "Oh." *Great. Go to Jail, Alice.* "Well, I'm out," she told them. "In jail and bankrupt."

"Ah, Mom," Alice whined. "You do that every time!"

"Well, it's between you and your dad now." She handed over her last bills to George, the banker. "I may take a shower and get ready for bed."

George reached out and touched her forearm. "Stay with us and watch the rest of the game. Will you?"

"Yeah, Mom. Please? We have had little time with you."

Ella was right, of course. "Okay. Sure." She looked down at George's fingertips, still grazing her wrist, and admitted to herself that his touch was nice. How often had he done that over the years of their marriage—the unconscious caress when he touched her?

He gradually pulled away, and Alice felt the disconnect. She glanced over the game board. "This has been nice. Family game time and dinner. The house felt so empty this summer."

George frowned. She knew what he was thinking. She was the one who suggested he leave.

"Along those lines," George said, "Ella and I looked at apartments this afternoon. No luck."

The tenderness just seconds earlier had now dissipated.

Alice shrugged. "It's okay. We'll stay in separate bedrooms for the next few days. Take your time, George. I'm going to be gone next week, anyway."

"Oh?"

Ella interjected. "It's beach week, Dad. Last week of August. Remember?"

"Right." He rolled the dice and then moved his marker three spaces. "Marilyn let you off for the week? Seems like a busy time right now for the campaign."

Alice exhaled. "I... I cut back on my campaign time. We hired a young man who is doing a fabulous job."

George stared and paused momentarily before responding. "I'm surprised." Then hesitantly, he added, "Do you want to tell me why?"

"I'm tiring of the campaign work, and honestly...?" She met his gaze. "A bit tired of Marilyn."

He sat still, studying her. "Oh. How so?"

"Well, for one, she wanted me to give up beach week."

He didn't miss a beat. "And heaven forbid you miss beach week."

"That's not fair, George."

He scooted his chair back, the legs squeaking against the wood plank flooring. "Really, Alice? It's the last week your daughter is home before heading back to school, and you won't spend it with her?"

Ella reached out to touch her dad's arm. "It's okay, Dad. Mom and I already talked about it."

"When?"

"Right after she got here."

George's head whipped around, and he glared at Alice. "Got it all worked out, huh?"

"No. Not really. But we talked about it briefly, and she's okay. Besides, we're inviting the younger girls for a day and night, so I'll get to spend time with her then."

"She's been gone all summer, Alice."

She stood, suddenly having had enough. "And whose decision was that? Ella wanted to be with you, George. That was her decision, and I respected her wishes."

"Like she had a choice."

"Of course I did, Dad."

Alice was suddenly furious. "What in the world! She *chose* to go with you. She could have stayed here, and we could have shared all kinds of experiences this summer. Instead, she went to the mountains with you. I had no say in the matter."

"Dad, she's right. Remember?"

He glanced sharply at Ella, then back at her. "Good Lord, Alice. With work and the campaign, you were never here!"

"Things changed."

"Mom. Dad. Stop."

George ignored Ella. "Oh, give me a break. Going to the cabin was a good thing. You've been working on that damned campaign all spring and summer. Plus, Marilyn has you on a tight leash in the mayor's office. When would you have had time for Ella or for me?"

"Well, that's a moot point now. Isn't it?"

"What do you mean?"

Alice shook her head. "Never mind. You'll find out soon enough."

"Excuse me?"

Ella shouted. "Mom, Dad, please stop! Someone is at the door!"

Alice glared at George. Where was his sudden anger coming from? "I'll get it."

With a huge sigh, she hustled down the hallway from the kitchen, wondering who would drop by at this hour. She flicked on the outside porch light, opened the door, and gasped.

"Marilyn? What in the world?" The last thing she wanted or needed right now was grief from her.

"Can we talk?"

She shook her head. "No. No. Not a good time."

"Look, Alice. The campaign is a mess. Matt is useless trying to get me ready for this debate, and the contract is all screwed up for Charlotte. I need you to forget this silly nonsense about quitting and get back to work."

Alice lifted her chin. "I've resigned, Marilyn. No."

"Will you open the door and come out here?"

George shouted from the kitchen. "Alice? Who is it?"

She glanced over her shoulder, then back to Marilyn. "I'm with my family this evening. I don't have time for this."

Marilyn grasped the screen door handle and jiggled it. Thank God it was locked from the inside, but her action perturbed Alice. *How dare she think she can open the door and walk right into my home?*

"Please?" she said. "I just want to say something."

"You can say it through the screen door."

She huffed. "Why are you being so pigheaded?"

"Pigheaded? Me?" Her voice pitched higher. "What the hell, Marilyn? You won't budge on anything once you've made up your mind."

"You can't quit."

"I already did. I am assuming you got my resignation letter."

"But what will you do?"

Alice laughed? "Do? What I've always done. Work. Take care of my family. Spend time with my friends."

"And me?"

George called out again. "Alice, is everything okay?"

"It's fine, George. I'll be right there."

"Are you back with him?" Marilyn asked. "Seriously?"

For the first time in her life, Alice had never felt so decisive. She might not yet know exactly what she wanted, but she knew what she didn't want any longer. "It's over. It's time to move on, Marilyn." *Find other prey.*

Marilyn jerked her head, as if in disbelief. "What does that mean?"

"That means we are through. You and me. I've wasted a lot of time waiting for our happily-ever-after, and it never came. I don't believe it ever will. And I don't intend to wait any longer to find out. You'll be fine without me, Marilyn. Now, go live your life, and I'll do the same."

"But Alice, I need you."

Ironic. And all this time you made me believe I needed you.

Alice stared into Marilyn's eyes and felt a little sorry for what she saw. Desperation. Loss. Confusion, perhaps. "No, you don't. You just think you do."

"No, Alice."

Where she found the strength to say her next words, she wasn't certain. "We're done, here. It's over. It never should have been. Good-bye, Marilyn."

Alice turned off the porch lamp. Marilyn's shocked expression faded with the light. Then slowly, but firmly, she shut the inside door.

She stood there for a moment, her palms flat against the cool wood, her fingers trembling, her mind swirling. Closing her eyes, she sighed, forcing out a breath she'd held for way too long.

Fourteen years. Wasted? No. She'd not think of it that way. She'd grown somewhat in those fourteen years. Hadn't she? For the good? Bad? Oh, she'd made mistakes along the way. Big ones. But all growth was beneficial, wasn't it?

If you learn from it?

And what had she learned?

Slowly, she pushed away, letting go of another lengthy breath. But she'd missed out on some things too—hadn't she? Was now the time to make up for all that?

She turned away from the door.

George stood a few feet down the hall, tears streaking his face.

"It's over," she whispered.

He opened his arms, and she closed the gap between them. His embrace had never felt so warm, or so welcome. The simple gesture told her all she needed to know.

He'd forgiven her.

Her heart ached with all the pain she'd caused him for way too long.

Seventeen

George snored softly next to her.

Alice woke slowly, staring at the filmy curtains lifting and falling in the early morning breeze at her bedroom window. The temperature and humidity had broken overnight, and she'd welcomed sleeping with the windows open. She lay there for a while, thinking over the past couple of days, until George's soft snores halted.

With a sigh, she turned and faced him—he was wide awake now. His dark eyes peered into hers, expressing his happiness waking up next to her.

"Good morning, sweetheart," he whispered. "How did you sleep?"

"Like a baby," she whispered. "I love sleeping with the windows open."

He grinned. "Oh, and is that the only reason you slept so well?" He leaned in with a soft kiss.

Alice nibbled his lips. "Oh, there. Could be. Another reason," she said between bites. "You, sir, wore me plumb out last night."

"And the night before?"

"And the one before that."

George's arm snaked around her back. He drew her closer, deepening the kiss, then slowly pulled away. "That is my intent. I want you happy, pleased, and satisfied. I want you in my bed and my life and—"

"Shush." Alice stopped him with a finger to his lips. "George, I *am* happy. I am here because I want to be. I choose you, George. You don't have to prove yourself to me. There is no competition going on here."

He sighed. "I just want to be what you need. What you want, Alice. All I've ever wanted was to make you happy. Somewhere along the line, I must have screwed up because...."

His words drifted and his eyes closed.

"George." Alice cupped his face with both her hands. "Please listen. You didn't screw up. None of this was your fault—it's all on me. But I love you, I swear it. I've always loved you, and I always will. Even when... Even when I wasn't *with* you. We shared so many years, so much of life. No one could ever compete with that. I'm here."

He let out another enormous sigh and gathered her next to his chest. "I love you, Alice McBain. These last couple of days... well, they've meant more than I could have asked for. You and Ella and me. The team. Back together again."

She kissed his chest. "Yes. The team."

They drifted into a dozy sleep for several minutes.

Downstairs, the doorbell rang. Alice glanced at the clock on the nightstand. "Who in the world? It's barely seven o'clock."

"I'll go see who it is," George said.

Alice stopped him, laying a palm on his chest. "No, you stay in bed and keep cozy." She kissed his lips. "I'll be right back, and then I have plans for you, mister."

His eyebrows waggled. Alice giggled.

The doorbell sounded again.

"Coming!"

She quickly pulled her nightgown over her head, slipped into her robe and tied the sash, then rushed down the stairs and opened the door.

Griff stood on the porch, a large mocha in hand.

Alice gulped. *No. Not now.*

"What in the world are you doing here?" she whispered.

He grinned wide and winked. "You haven't been by for a few days for your mocha, so I thought I'd deliver."

She glanced back at the stairwell. "I don't understand."

He stepped closer. "Are you avoiding me, Alice?"

"I don't know what you are talking about." Of course, that was a lie. She knew perfectly well what he was referring to.

Griff laughed. "Oh, I get it. You're playing hard to get now. Right. That could be fun." He pushed the mocha toward the door. "Take this before it gets cold."

"I don't want it, Griff. You should go."

He stood planted on the porch, studying her. "What gives, Alice? I thought we had a thing going here. We had fun, didn't we? You seemed to enjoy yourself. I had heard you weren't working for Marilyn anymore, so I figured things were still rocky with the two of you. And then I thought, perhaps Alice needs a little morning boost to get her day started." He winked.

And he wasn't talking about the mocha.

Alice gripped the door and started to slam it, then stopped herself. "Go to hell, Griff, and get off my porch. Take your mocha with you."

Griff shrugged, glancing behind her. "Your loss. Maybe I'll drop by another day when you're a little more needy. You know, like you were the other night when you showed up at my apartment and stayed the night." He paused, then pulled something out of his back pocket. "Oh, and by the way, you forgot this."

The bra she'd left behind dangled from his fingertips.

Her cheeks heated. "Look, Griff. What happened was a mistake. It won't, can't, happen again. And you cannot show up here unannounced like this expecting—"

"Expecting what?" George stepped up behind her, looking out the door. "What the hell are you doing here, Griff?" Then he looked at Alice. "And what the hell are you not telling me?"

Eighteen

BEACH WEEK, SATURDAY

BEACH THERAPY IS NOW IN SESSION.

Alice couldn't help but let those words roll through her head as she settled onto the sofa at Tequila Sunrise. She knew that eventually the subject of her sleeping with Griff would come up.

Little did they know, Griff was just the tip of the iceberg.

"Alright. One margarita, two margaritas, three margaritas, four." Julia claimed the last one for herself because it had a wedge of orange, rather than a lemon or lime. That was their signal for the week—an orange slice meant the drink was non-alcoholic and reserved for her.

Alice was so proud of Julia and her sobriety journey. She was just as proud of the rest of them for doing everything possible to make Julia feel comfortable with their drinking.

Of course, Julia took it all in stride.

It was afternoon, and they'd all arrived at Tequila Sunrise, their favorite beach house—compliments of Lia and Zach.

Alice lifted her margarita and leaned back on the cushions, drawing her legs up under her. Maggie sat to her right. Julia and Lia were seated across from them, on the other side of the large square coffee table. Outside the floor-to-ceiling windows and doors was the deck, and beyond that and over the dune, the beach. She couldn't wait until morning to take an early walk along the shore—that always helped to center her day.

But first, some beach therapy.

"Lia, please tell Zach thanks for letting us have the house for free this year. I don't think any of us expected that."

"I know," Lia said. "That's for all time now. Okay? Isn't it nice that we don't have to worry about that expense any longer? Now that Zach and I own the house, all we need to worry about is reserving the space. And honestly, I'm pretty sure Belle has already booked the last week of August out for at least ten years."

"Well," Maggie said, "we appreciate it. But you know that means that one of us is buying your dinner every night."

"That's right." Julia lifted her fake margarita. "It's the least we can do."

Alice agreed. "Absolutely."

The room quieted while everyone sipped their drinks. Then Lia suggested something. "I was wondering, ladies, if you would like to try something. How about if we unplug for a few days. You know, do a social media cleanse? Maybe we can try it for a day, and then if we like it, we can do more."

Maggie stared at her, holding her phone. "You mean, like, no cell phones? I have kids...."

"Right." Lia nodded. "And all our kids and families are safe and taken care of, plus they all know where we are and there is a landline here in case of emergencies. Let's just unplug from the world and... well, just be."

Julia slapped her phone face down on the coffee table. "I'm in. I say we text our people now, saying we are unplugging, and give them the emergency number should they need it."

"Great idea." Lia started texting.

"But wait. We haven't all agreed!" Maggie said.

"I think it's a super idea." Alice actually would welcome no contact with anyone for the rest of the week, especially Marilyn. And she doubted that George and Ella would even attempt to contact her, so there was that. "I'm in."

Lia trotted off to the kitchen, then came back with a basket and a slip of paper. "Okay, send your last text. Here's the emergency number from the fridge. Then park your phones in the basket."

Maggie whimpered a little.

Alice thought it comical. "Oh, come on, Maggie. It will be okay."

"All right. Fine." She blew out a breath that made her cheeks puff out.

They texted. They parked the phones. And Lia whisked the basket off to...somewhere, and then looked at Maggie. "So," she said after a minute. "When do your kids go back to school, Maggie?"

Alice recognized Lia's ploy of distraction and gave her a wink.

Lia grinned back.

Maggie took a breath, then another sip of her margarita. "Right after Labor Day. And oh, that reminds me, we're checking out of the Gull early next week."

"Oh?" Lia looked surprised.

"Yes. We need to get back to Rocky Mount. All the kids need school clothes—they've grown so much over the summer—plus Carol needs to shop for college. I want us settled before school starts. And once all that is done, I need to think about selling the house."

Julia leaned in. "You've decided to sell?"

Maggie nodded. "I think so. Lots of memories there, and most of them are not good. Besides, downsizing is not a bad idea."

"I think you're smart," Lia said.

"Ditto." Alice was curious. "With Carol headed off to college, your nest is getting emptier. When do you take her to ECU?"

"Honestly, I need to check with her about when. I think the week before Labor Day. Does that sound right? What about Ella?"

Alice sighed. "Sounds about right. Ella is...complicated." She lied, and it probably showed all over her face.

"Oh?" Maggie stared at her, as if waiting for further explanation.

Not happening. Not now. She waved off the question. "We can talk more later."

"Well," Julia interrupted. "Hannah is flying in tomorrow. Sam is ecstatic she's coming. I'm happy they will get some quality time together."

"That's awesome news, Julia. I can't wait to see all the girls together," Lia said.

"It will be fun for them, and for us," Maggie added.

Alice nodded. *Sure.* "Right."

Again, the conversation lulled.

"So, Alice." Maggie turned her way. "We've not touched base since our lunch. How did the week go now that George and Ella are back from the mountains? And...dare I ask...what about this Griff person? Any word there?"

And there it is.

Alice made brief eye contact with each of her friends, unsure whether to dive in, or ease them in slowly. On impulse, she simply started talking but honestly wasn't certain how far she wanted to take the conversation right yet.

"My life is a total train wreck. I have royally fucked up."

Maggie reached for her hand and squeezed. Lia and Julia set their drinks aside and leaned forward.

"Just tell us," Julia coaxed. "Let it go."

"You're sure?"

They all nodded.

"Well... Alright." She set her drink on the coffee table, too, and scooted to the end of her sofa cushion. Closing her eyes, she thought back to the beginning of her hellish week. "Let me recall a few things first, to orient myself, because this entire week has been a blur."

Maggie patted her hand. "Take your time."

How did I get myself into this predicament? I'm always the one patting hands, and holding back hair, and listening to their woes. When did the tables turn?

"So, you know what happened Monday night. Griff."

"Yes."

"Then, George and Ella were home the next morning, and I had lunch with all of you later."

"Right."

"And I went home after *that*—thanks to Julia for seeing me home —and George was fixing dinner. He was just so...good. Seemed genuinely happy to see me. And I felt so guilty. Oh, George. He doesn't deserve any of this!" She sniffed and Maggie kept patting her hand. "Anyway, we did dinner. Then we had family game night. George kept saying he wanted normal, you know? So, we had *normal* that night. Ella loved it. He loved it. I loved it. I thought, maybe, it could be the start of us mending, healing, and perhaps even getting back to being a family again." She paused for a moment. No one said a word. "And then...."

She stopped, staring at the table.

"And then...?" Julia prodded.

"Well, then, all hell broke loose."

"Oh, Alice." Maggie pulled her closer and laid her head on her shoulder. "I'm so sorry."

Alice let out a breath. "You know? I want to talk about this eventually. All of it. What happened. How I'm feeling. My confusion about my sexuality... But not yet."

"Too soon?" Lia asked.

She nodded. "I need a little more time."

"You got it," Julia told her. "We have all week."

THE AFTERNOON SAILED ON, WITH EVERYONE GETTING settled in their rooms, plus some lazy lounging on the deck. Later, they had drinks and dinner at The Whale's Tail, a popular Carolina seafood and steak place on the sound side of Tuckaway Bay. They argued over who would pick up Lia's dinner, then eventually settled on a plan for the week.

Julia paid for her dinner that night. Lia would tomorrow. Alice the next night. They'd start all over again on Tuesday.

Alice was unusually quiet throughout the dinner, while her friends chattered on about this and that. The thought of telling them about breaking it off with Marilyn, the second fiasco with Griff, and that she was definitely on the outs with George and Ella, was a bit of a heavy lift for her at the moment—and she wanted to be mentally prepared.

When she talked, she figured there'd be crying, something she'd not yet let herself do—because she was pretty sure she'd lost any hope of remaining friends with George, forever, and she was damned uncertain about how Ella felt.

She had to prepare herself for all that. Fortunately, she had the week, and the girlfriends, to help her figure it out.

What she wasn't prepared for, however—*none of them were*—was coming back to Tequila Sunrise from dinner and finding their AWOL friends, Wren and Willow, waiting for them on the deck. It had been two years since they'd seen them.

"Surprise!" The twins shouted.

The six women rushed together, giggling and shouting.

"But how?" Lia asked, holding Wren at arm's length. "And where have you been? Can you tell us?"

The twins exchanged a glance. Alice knew right then and there that the forthcoming information was going to be sparse.

"We can tell you a little," Wren said. "Not much." Then she subtly pointed to a man by the dune. "See that guy over there?"

"Yes?" Lia said.

Julia intervened with a hand to Wren's arm. "He's a cop. I can tell. Undercover."

Willow took a breath. "Yeah." She glanced about, then whispered, "We're in witness protection."

Alice wasn't sure she'd heard correctly. "Seriously? Like in the movies. Is he like, your handler or something?"

Willow bit her lip, a seemingly insecure gesture, which Alice found rather interesting. "Something like that. He's kind of our bodyguard for today, and he'll have to stay in the house tonight. Hope that's okay."

Alice glanced at the guy. "Is he available?" He was cute. *Yeah, Alice. Why not fuck your life up even more? Make it three men in a week? Oh, good God. Grow up!*

Wren laughed. "I thought you were married?"

Julia scoffed. "Yesterday's news."

"I'm getting a divorce," Alice said.

She said it with conviction, and she could tell that it wasn't lost on Julia, Lia, and Maggie. They all gave her a blank look.

Willow laughed. "Alice, you tart you!"

Julia snorted. "Tart? You have no idea. She is leaving George for a woman."

"Get the fuck out of town!" Willow said loudly.

"It's true." Alice said. *Sort of. Not.* But they didn't know that yet, so she'd play along, for now. "Can you stay all week?" Alice asked. Honestly, she'd love the distraction and to shift the focus off her.

"Just tonight. We have to leave in the morning."

"Then what *can* you tell us?"

Alice noted Julia edging closer, curious. Being a lawyer, she got into investigative stuff.

"Can I help in any way?" Julia queried.

Again, the twins made eye contact. "Let's go inside," Wren said. "It is getting late." She lowered her voice then and added, "We can talk more after we get settled."

Alice watched Willow motion to the guy sitting on the dune steps. He stood and walked toward them.

Maggie's eyes went big as saucers, ogling the guy. Alice had to laugh internally.

They came into the house, and the bodyguard locked the door behind them. "Mind if I close these drapes?" he asked.

"Of course not," Lia said. "No problem."

He checked the locks on the two sliding doors, closed the drapes, then went to the kitchen and checked the windows there and then the back door. "I'd like to go upstairs to make sure everything is secure."

Alice suddenly felt a little uneasy. "Is that necessary?"

"Yes, ma'am. It is."

Willow stepped forward. "I'm sorry, you all. He needs to clear the house. He already checked the perimeter. Oh, and by the way, his name is Brad."

"Hey Brad," Maggie said, a sassy grin on her face.

Julia softly punched her on the bicep.

Brad gave a professional nod to the women, then headed upstairs.

Turning, Julia said, "What the hell, Willow? What's going on? And I know his name isn't Brad. What's with the secretive fuckery?"

Wren exhaled hard and grasped Julia's hand. "Let's sit. All of us. Okay?"

Brad skipped down the stairs and faced them. "All clear. If you ladies want to stake a claim upstairs and do your girl thing, that would be great. I'll stay down here and man the entrances and exits."

Wren nodded. "I think that sounds like a plan."

"Yes," Willow echoed. "Shall we take snacks?"

"Definitely," Lia said.

"And booze," Maggie added, then glanced at Julia. "And oranges."

Julia laughed. "Right."

Willow narrowed her gaze. "Why is that funny?"

"Oh, girl," Julia said, nudging Willow. "We have so much to catch up on."

<hr>

THE BEDROOM AT THE BACK OF THE HOUSE WAS THE largest, so they all settled in there. Brad helped them with snacks, a cooler, and bottles of alcohol. They weren't restricted to upstairs, by any means, he told them. They could always jog down for refills. They also made sure he had plenty of snacks downstairs.

The room had two double beds, with plenty of space in between, and a large window facing the ocean. They set up their bar on the dresser, snacks on a blanket on the floor, and gathered up pillows and blankets from the other rooms.

No one held any expectations about sleeping that night.

"What time do you have to leave, girls?" Julia asked.

Wren frowned. "By seven in the morning."

"Well, shit."

"Then before we go any further," Maggie added, "spill it, women. We need details. Where the hell have you been for the past two years?"

The twins looked at each other, then Wren spoke. "We discussed this ahead of time because we knew you would want answers, and we also knew there was only so much we could say. Right now, anyway."

Willow nodded her way. "Yes. The fact is, we don't want to tell you much because the more you know, the more risk for all of you. We even debated coming here to see you because we do not want to drag any of you into our mess."

"But you came anyway?" Alice thought Wren looked worried.

"Yes," she said. "For two reasons. We miss you, and we want you to know that we are okay."

"But you can't give us details."

"No."

Willow glanced at Wren, scooted closer to everyone, and lowered her voice. "But here's what we can tell you." She sighed. "It's been a long couple of years. My business is in trouble, and I pissed some people off. Important people who have power. I can't tell you who, because you might recognize names, so I won't. Wren got dragged into this unknowingly, but at least we are together and protected. Brad down there? He's a U.S. Marshal. We're in the Witness Protection Program, on our way to provide statements to law enforcement, and we asked to stop over here for a quick visit. We were surprised when they said yes."

"That's kind of unusual." Julia leaned toward Willow. "Where are you going?"

"I can't tell you."

Julia slowly nodded. "Of course."

"So, if you can't talk about that, Willow," Lia said, "can you tell us where you have been?"

Wren interjected. "We were separated for over a year, in hiding. We have a secret way of communicating—have since we were teenagers—so we could keep in touch. I lived on an island in the Atlantic for a while, but I moved around a lot. Willow was with Spence in another country. The past year we've been together, and in the program, because of—"

"Wren. No." Willow gave her a look of caution.

"Right," she said. "Honestly, that's about it. Sorry."

"Wait. One more question," Lia said. "Do you have new identities?"

The twins exchanged glances again. "Sort of."

"You can't tell us," Julia said.

Wren nodded. "But as soon as we can, we will."

Willow agreed. "But what about all of you? What's happened with everyone while we were away?"

Julia laughed. "Oh, you have no idea."

Wren's face illuminated. "Tell us!"

Lia put her hands up—Alice guessed to signal she was going to take this. "Let me just summarize it for you," she said. "Ready?"

"Absolutely."

"So, Julia went to rehab because she's an alcoholic, and now she's sober. She's living with a guy named Sam here on the island. She and Mark are divorced and he married their B&B manager. Maggie filed for divorce, but then Max died before it was final. A lot of bad shit happened in between. Right before Max died, she found out he had a baby mama and a little boy in Australia. So, her kids now have a sibling. As for me? Zach and I got married, inherited the resort, and Belle had a baby during a Christmas Eve nor'easter on the food prep island. Whew. That pretty much sums it up, except for Alice."

Alice felt all eyes turn her way.

"And honestly, Alice, I wasn't sure what you wanted me to tell."

She shrugged. "Well, that's because you can't, Lia. You haven't heard half the story yet."

The group fell silent. A few seconds passed.

"Alright, Alice," Willow said. "Spill it. What the fuck is going on with you?"

She spanned the room, eyeballing her friends. "Alright, ladies. Get your drinks ready."

It didn't take her long to get Wren and Willow up to speed, sharing what the other women already knew. She told them about Marilyn, and their long-term affair, and how she and George had finally agreed to an amicable divorce. She also shared about Carol and Ella arguing at Christmas, and Carol spilling the beans about Alice being gay. Then she explained why she asked George to leave for the summer. Somewhere along the line, she also mentioned the campaign, working for Marilyn, and all of that, too.

"So then, this past Monday, the dam burst."

"What happened?" Wren asked.

"I happened. I screwed up. Marilyn pissed me off. I resigned my job with the campaign. And then I went straight to this guy I know, his name is Griff—who sort of came onto me earlier in the day—and I spent the night with him."

"Wait," Willow said. "You had sex? With a man. But I thought...."

"Yes. I did. Right?"

"But you're gay."

"I suppose. I'm still questioning a lot of things about my sexuality."

"Oh, Alice." Wren reached out and gave her a hug. "I'm so sorry."

She shrugged. "Who would think at my age? I should have this shit figured out by now."

"I really don't think it's all that uncommon, Alice," Julia said. "Maybe have a chat with Hannah while she's here. You know she specializes in LGBTQ+ concerns."

Willow tilted her head. "Hannah?"

Julia nodded. "Oh, right. She's Sam's daughter, and a future psychologist. My bonus stepdaughter, sort of. She'll be here later in the week."

Alice wasn't sure she wanted to talk to Hannah. Goodness, she had twenty years on the girl. But she was a psychologist and gay herself, so.... "I might. Thanks for that idea, Julia."

"But you know we are all here, too," Julia added.

"And we have broad shoulders for listening," Wren told her.

"I know. This whole ordeal... It's my own damn fault, though." Pausing for a moment, she took a breath. "Of course, me sleeping with George also screwed things up."

They all stared at her.

Willow shot up and poured herself another shot of tequila. "Get the fuck out of town."

"But not before I broke up with Marilyn," Alice added.

"I think *I'm* confused," Wren said. "Willow, get me one of those."

"Coming."

"Join the club. Confusion is my middle name," Alice told her. "We had a nice evening that night—George, Ella, and me. And then Marilyn came knocking at the door. She wanted me to come back to work. I told her no. And just to make a long story short, that's when I cut it off with her for good."

Lia gasped. "You broke up? After all these years? How many, actually?"

"Oh, fourteenish." Alice nodded. "Yes. I told her we were through."

"Oh, Alice." Maggie scooted closer. "Are you okay?"

She met Maggie's gaze. "I'm fine about that. It should have happened long ago." Then she looked at the others. "George overheard me tell her it was over. And when I turned around, all I could see were his tears and his open arms. I went back to him."

Maggie sat up straight. "You're back with George?"

"Oh my God, Alice," Lia said. "That's fantastic news." She hesitated. "Isn't it?"

She shook her head. "No. I'm *not* back with George. Well, I was, for two days, and everything was good. Things were great with Ella, too. It was like old times."

Julia stood, picking up her drink. "But it's not now though, right? You said two days...."

"Right."

Maggie leaned into her shoulder. "So, let me get this straight. You quit your job, broke up with Marilyn, slept with Griff, and then you slept with George, too? All in the same week?"

Alice glanced sideways at Maggie, whose eyes were wide with question. "What do you think?"

"I, uh... I think you did."

"And you would be right." Alice stood then, leaving her drink behind, and focused on the dune behind the deck. "George and I had three wonderful nights."

"That's a helluva lot of stress," Julia said.

"And then...?" Maggie prodded. "What happened next?"

She steadied her gaze. "And then yesterday morning, Griff came to the house carrying a mocha coffee and my bra, suggesting another romp in the sack. George overheard him."

"Shit."

"I don't like Griff anymore," Lia said. "I always thought he was nice."

Alice shrugged. "Not his fault. I pursued him. Why wouldn't he think I might want another go at it? Anyway, it's moot, because I sent him packing, and now George is gone. Ella, too."

"Back to the mountains?" Maggie asked.

She faced her. "No. They packed up Ella's things to move back to school. They left for ECU this morning, right before I came here. Ella and George decided she needed an apartment this year, so they are working on renting something, and he's staying until she's settled. He also spoke of moving closer to her, because apparently, there are a ton of open teaching positions in the area."

"But school starts back the week after next here."

"Right." Alice nodded. "So, he'll come back, I assume, unless he finds another job."

"But wait." Julia met Alice's gaze. "Does that mean Ella isn't coming this Thursday?"

To be candid, Alice hadn't even thought about that. She sighed. "I honestly don't know, Julia. I didn't even think to ask her."

Lia went to her and put an arm around her shoulders. "It's okay, Alice. It will all work out."

Who is playing mother hen now?

They all stopped talking. Alice watched their faces. Julia's gaze was fixed on her. Lia hugged her a little tighter. Maggie sat staring ahead. Wren and Willow honestly looked shell-shocked. They'd just had a lot thrown at them.

"I'm okay," she said softly. "It's an adjustment. I'll be fine. I need to figure out things, you know? Who I am?"

"We're here. You know that," Lia said.

"I wish we could stay longer, Alice," Wren said, "To be here for you."

"Just know we support you and all of your decisions," Willow added.

"That goes for all of us." Maggie nodded.

"I know that. But this week? I've got some soul-searching to do."

"Beach therapy. Good for what ails you," Julia said.

Alice agreed. "Yes. But I might need you all to hold *my* hair back, for once." She knew they understood she was speaking figuratively, not literally. She'd never been puking drunk in her life.

"Oh, Alice." Lia fully embraced her

Julia and Maggie joined them. Wren and Willow leaned in, too.

"We've got you, sweetie," Julia said.

"Always," Maggie added.

Nineteen

They slept most of the day on Sunday after Wren and Willow left, and even once they were all awake, ventured no further than the beach house deck. Dinner was Chinese delivery, stale snacks, and whatever alcohol remained.

They'd probably need to make a tequila run later today.

Alice rose early Monday morning, unable to sleep any longer. She slipped into a loose sundress, grabbed her sunhat and flip-flops, and headed for the deck. Her goal was to catch the sunrise from the dune walkover, then head out for her morning walk.

She had a few moments of semi-darkness sitting there, the morning still and the ocean calm. The outside lights from the surrounding houses lit up certain areas of the beach. A few gulls cried out, as if saying good morning, and an occasional ghost crab skittered to its hole below.

She needed the quiet. *This* quiet. Right now.

Needed to clear her head of the clamor—some of it coming from herself, some from others. Things said. She knew that until she could release the chatter to the universe, clearing her head of the noise, could her heart understand what to do next.

Only then would she know what to do.

A few streaks of yellow and orange burst up over the distant horizon, and Alice stood to watch. Shielding her eyes with her hand, she waited as the colors morphed into existence, pulling in the varying hues of a color wheel. Then, the yellow orb burst over the water, shooting rays of pink and lavender and blue-gray skyward.

She donned her sunhat, took the steps to the shore, and let the cool waters drift over her toes, leaving bubbles and froth behind. She ambled without purpose or direction, unsure how far she'd walked. Didn't matter. No one to worry about. No one to get home to.

No one to take care of.

Time to take care of you, Alice. Time to make yourself the priority.

She was free—free to make her own decisions and plot out the next few minutes of her life—and then, very soon, the direction she wanted to take her life.

Looking up, she realized she'd wandered all the way to Quigley Pier, so she headed in for some coffee and a doughnut, chatted with some locals for a while, then headed back toward Tequila Sunrise.

She gathered a few rocks and shells along the way, and then about halfway home, ran into Maggie.

"Mind if I join you?"

Alice smiled. "Sure. I don't mind company."

They walked in silence for a bit, each picking at things in the sand. After a while, Alice spotted a larger item a few feet ahead, perhaps a conch shell, gently nestled in the sand. She jogged ahead to snag the thing before the sea reclaimed it.

When she got there, she realized it was a rock, not a shell. She collected it anyway, wiping the grit away. It was gray, sea-worn, and smooth...and shaped like a crooked heart.

She glanced behind her. "Hey Maggie. Look what I found."

Maggie strolled closer. "A heart-shaped rock! That's pretty neat."

"Yeah. I like it."

Maggie smiled. "It's cool." She studied her. "You okay this morning?"

"I'm okay." She grinned. "I got a good night's sleep, and that's a good thing."

"Me too."

They walked in silence for a while. Alice could tell Maggie was holding back something. Finally, she asked her. "Is there something you want to say?"

She turned quickly and gave Alice a hug. "Just that... Oh, Alice. I know we've not always seen eye-to-eye, and then there was all the crap at Christmas with Carol, but you were there so much for me when I needed my people. And I want you to know that should you need to talk, or need me for anything else, I'm here. Anytime. Even after I'm back in Rocky Mount."

Maggie's sincerity touched her. It was true they'd had their share of spats and disagreements—much of it over lifestyle and their daughters—but Alice knew one thing for certain, all of her Tuckaway Bay girls were there for each other, no matter what.

"I do know that, Maggie."

"Good."

Enough said. They strolled along quietly for several more yards, Tequila Sunrise a short walk down the beach now.

"Sometimes, you know," Alice said, "it helps just having someone beside you. Words don't always have to be said. Just knowing someone else is there, means everything."

Maggie smiled wide, her face animated. "Thank you for saying that."

"You're welcome."

She glanced at Alice's hand holding the rock. "I have an idea. Could I borrow your rock for a while? Maybe a day or two? I promise to give it back."

"The heart rock? I was thinking of tossing it back into the ocean."

Maggie shook her head. "Oh no. I have an idea. Let me take it. Please?"

Alice shrugged and handed it over to Maggie, who looked like she'd just been given a pot of gold.

"Anyone interested in heading up to Duck today? Looks like some sort of festival going on at the Scarborough Faire

Shopping Village." Julia stood in the kitchen, reading an advertisement. "I haven't been to their bookstore in a while."

Wednesday mornings were always the best mornings at Tequila Sunrise, Alice thought. They'd recovered from the initial weekend binge of food and drink, and a couple of lazy days of deck sunning. They'd slept in a few mornings by now and were ready to get out of the house—perhaps take a day trip somewhere or go shopping.

"Oh, I like that place." Alice looked over her shoulder at the flyer. "So cute and cozy, tucked back in under those trees. Where did that flyer come from?"

"I think it was an ad from someone's food delivery."

"Coffee's ready!" Lia shouted.

"Great. I need a bucket of it." Julia deposited the paper on the counter and started across the room but halted abruptly, looking out onto the deck. "Ugh. Those damn seagulls. Who left food outside last night?" She opened the sliding door. "Go! Shoo!"

"I think Maggie ordered pizza late." Lia filled a coffee cup.

With a sigh, Julia closed the door and turned back. "Maggie!"

"She's still asleep." Alice padded over to the coffeemaker. "Julia, give me your bucket and I'll fill it up."

"Ha!"

Maggie lumbered down the stairs. "Who's yelling at me?"

"I am," Julia said. "You left pizza out on the deck."

"Oh crap. I didn't. I was so tired. I actually fell asleep in the lounge chair." She shuffled to the window and looked out. "Crap."

"Yeah. Crap."

"There's a hose at the side of the house. It will reach up to the deck," Lia told her.

"I'll take care of it." She faced the girls. "But can I have coffee first?"

"Of course."

Julia rifled through the cabinets and produced two more cups, an oversized one for her, and another for Maggie. She set them on the counter, and Alice poured. These women were something else first thing in the morning.

"Yum," Maggie said, settling herself at the large table. "Life in a cup."

"Good Lord." Julia laughed.

Maggie sipped again and sighed. "Someone's phone is pinging. A lot. Can you all hear that? Where's that basket?"

Lia approached the table, setting her cup down. "You're right. Damn you have good hearing."

"Someone is persistent." Maggie twisted toward the sound. "And it's too early for that shit."

"They'll call the landline if it's an emergency," Lia reminded her. "It's all good, Maggie."

At that moment, the landline phone rang.

All four women jumped.

Julia was the closest, so she grabbed it, watching the other three. "Hello?" She paused, listening, then looked directly at Alice.

A thud of worry landed in the pit of her gut, and a weird sensation crawled up her spine. Alice's heart fluttered and her breath caught.

Something is wrong. OMG. Ella. George?

"Alright, Zach," Julia said into the phone. "Thanks. I'll tell Alice, and we'll check our phones and...."

Her voice trailed off and Alice heard nothing else.

Lia raced into the kitchen area, dragging a chair with her. She climbed up to a high cabinet and pulled down the basket.

Alice got there first and snatched up her phone. Her fingers trembled as she punched in her passcode and scrolled. She thought she might throw up her coffee. "What the fuck am I looking for, Julia!"

"Check your texts, email. Anything about the campaign?"

What? "I don't care about the fricking campaign. Are my people okay?"

"Alice." Maggie stood beside her.

"Is it Ella? Did something happen? George?" She fumbled and dropped her phone. "Dammit!"

"Stop." Maggie grabbed Alice's arm. "Oh, fucking shit, Alice?"

She froze and looked at Maggie's face. Her friend stared back, worry reflected in her eyes. Fear gripped Alice's throat, and she wasn't sure she could even speak. "What. Is it?"

Maggie slowly turned her phone around so Alice could see a news website up on her browser. She had apparently hit a link from somewhere, or from someone, sending her to an article on the Slant Politics blog. The photo at the top of the news article was of her and Marilyn, embraced and kissing, on the deck of the hotel in Buxton.

Slant Politics.

The national conservative online political rag.

Holy fucking shit.

As if George finding out about her tryst with Griff wasn't problematic enough, that article was likely the final nail in her marital coffin.

The pictures of her and Marilyn had surfaced.

The secret she'd hidden for over fourteen years was now public knowledge.

***

ALICE GASPED AND SANK INTO A CHAIR BY THE TABLE, panting, trembling. "Dizzy."

Chest tight. Shaking.

Can't. Get. Air.

Lia was next to her. "Put your head down. You'll hyperventilate."

Her world was spinning. Out of control. On multiple levels.

Falling. Melting into the floor.

"She's going down. Grab her!"

Lia. Saying things. Julia on the phone? Maggie's hands, on her shoulders?

"Alice. Breathe into this bag."

The paper crowded up against her mouth. Someone held it. She huffed.

"Come on, Alice. Breathe deep. Head down."

She did. Seemingly for hours. Her breathing finally slowed and narrowed. Her head cleared, somewhat. "Answer those damn phones." Her shaking hand stroked her temple.

Headache.

Lia helped her stand. Maggie on the other side. "In a minute. Let's get you to the sofa."

She steadied herself, letting them guide her there, closing her eyes for a moment after she sat. When she opened them, Julia faced her, sitting on the edge of the coffee table. "Be still for a minute, let your body recover and relax."

"Is this a...panic attack? Anxiety? 'Cause I don't like it."

"Yes, likely a panic attack."

Maggie sat beside her. "But you're allowed one, Alice. Here, take this." She placed a tiny pill in her hand.

"What are you giving her, Maggie?" Julia said sternly.

"Relax, Julia. It's a Xanax. I have a prescription and it might help."

Alice pushed Maggie's hand away and shook her head. "No. Thanks, but I don't need that. I'm fine."

Julia nodded to Maggie, then said to Alice. "Try to breathe normally, okay?"

She closed her eyes again. Could better focus, center herself that way.

Maggie clasped her hand.

After a moment, her brain churned again with questions. "What do we know?"

"Not much," Julia said. "I called Zach back. He apparently overheard the chatter in the restaurant about the pictures, so he started searching online. Seems that *Slant* is the only place that has posted... But Alice, apparently the network news stations have picked it up and are teasing it on social media."

Alice stared off. *Great.* "Refresh my memory because I'm still a little fuzzy. I didn't tell you about the pictures, did I?"

Julia glanced from Lia to Maggie, then back to Alice again. "No, you didn't. Do you want to?"

"Yes." She leaned into Maggie a little. "They surfaced a few weeks ago. It's the reason why my job was terminated at the mayor's office, and why Marilyn resigned as mayor. Basically, we were blackmailed by Faust's minions who were apparently planted in the Tuckaway Bay government system to get some dirt on Marilyn. There could be more to that. I don't know. Seems they found their dirt—or their interpretation of dirt—anyway."

"You said blackmailed. What exactly happened?" Julia held her gaze.

"It was one of those resign or we go to the press things. So, I was sacked, and then Marilyn resigned and spun the story her way. Remember the first presser at the new headquarters? It was that day. We thought it was done, but apparently not. She's moving up in the polls, so maybe Faust decided to act. I don't have a clue... Speculation here."

Julia looked off into the kitchen. "Who else knew about the pictures?"

She shrugged. "No one, that I know of." Then she remembered. "Wait. I think Marilyn said her husband had copies."

"Interesting. Would he have released them?"

Alice didn't think so. "I think if Marilyn thought he would, she would have been more panicked about that. No, pretty sure it was from Faust."

"What about George?"

"Oh, no. I didn't tell him. Shit. I need my phone."

Julia leaned in. "Alice, I'd advise you not to read too much or dig too deep. Let us filter information to you."

"No. I need my phone." She started to stand, then abruptly sat back down. Still woozy.

"Alice," Julia continued, "I don't think that's wise."

"I need to call George."

Lia had already retrieved her phone from the kitchen table. "Here. Seems yours is the one blowing up."

Great. She unlocked the device and immediately scanned the notifications. Texts. Calls. Emails.

Three calls and three voicemails from Marilyn. Alice listened to none of them.

Too many texts to count. A few from Zach. One from Matt. And an ungodly number from Marilyn. She scrolled on.

Her email inbox was full of political news, most featuring headlines about Marilyn.

The Senatorial Candidate's Lesbian Lover
City Officials Fired Over Love Triangle
Faust Calls for Morgan to Resign Amidst Affair Scandal
Morgan's Liberal Agenda, A Step Too Far
What The Husband's Think. Or Do They Care?

She read no more.

There was nothing from George or Ella.

She dialed his number. No answer.

Frowning, she tried Ella. No answer there either. *Text me,* her mailbox recording said, *Talking is so Gen X.*

She sought Julia's gaze. "What do I do now? Do I talk to Marilyn? Go down there? To the campaign headquarters. I'm sure she's frantic, but I really don't want to."

Julia shook her head. "Stay here. Inside. No one knows you're here. Right? This is your safe place. We all lie low until we get more information and come up with a plan. In the meantime, talk to no one."

"Right. I can do that."

"I'm going to explore the legal aspects. I have a paralegal back in Louisville who is a whiz at deep research. We need to know what legal rights you have and your best next steps. This is an invasion of your privacy."

Someone pounded at the kitchen door, the one facing the road.

"Don't answer it," Julia warned.

The person knocking shouted. "Alice! Let me in, please!"

"It's Marilyn." She felt a little sorry for her. Sitting up, she wrang her hands. "I should go to her."

"No talking until you get your act together and know what you want to say." Julia glanced at the door. "I hate to leave her out there like that, but honestly, you need to consider how this affects you, and I don't want her viewpoint to cloud your decisions."

Alice took a breath. "Right."

The pounding again. "Alice! Please! I know you are in there."

"God, she sounds desperate," Maggie said.

Lia glanced toward the door. "Wouldn't you be, too?"

"I suppose."

Suddenly, the gulls created a ruckus on the deck again, squawking and flapping, drawing the women's attention away from Marilyn.

"What the...?" Julia rose. "Fucking shit."

Half a dozen reporters with phones and cameras ready were crawling over the deck, sending the gulls flying. They shouted into the house, their faces pressed against the glass windows and doors.

"Alice McBain! Can we get a statement?"

"What's the current status of your relationship with Marilyn Morgan, Ms. McBain?"

"How long has this affair been going on?"

"Will you advise Marilyn to drop from the race?"

Julia and Maggie raced to shut the curtains.

Lia let Marilyn in the back door.

Twenty

The women immediately churned into action—except for Alice, who could only sit and watch from the far side of the great room. Her brain still reeled from trying to catch up on the consequences of everything going down.

Lia had called Zach, who promptly came and told the news crews they were trespassing on private property and to stay on the public beach. Any place past the bottom of the beachside dune steps, he told them, was off limits. His maintenance crew helped to strongly convince the reporters that they needed to comply. The men stayed on the deck, and currently, Lia was outside with them.

Julia contacted the local police, who arrived a few minutes after Zach and supported his trespassing statement. As an attorney, Julia apparently had some idea of how to handle these situations, and Alice was grateful. She convinced the officer to secure a marked car parked at the end of the driveway, and insisted that no one enter unless they cleared that person through her.

So, both accesses—to the front and rear of the house—were now secure. The only way anyone could get to them was from the houses on either side, and both were rented out to families. Julia had the officer alert the property owners and guests of the situation.

Maggie had turned on the television—something they rarely did at the beach—and was monitoring any "breaking news" situations with the sound turned down.

Marilyn paced the room, her arms crossed tightly over her chest, not saying much of anything.

Finally, Alice asked her to sit. "We should talk."

"I know." Marilyn halted and met her gaze. "I'm so sorry I got you into this mess."

"It's our mess. And I got into it willingly."

Marilyn shook her head. "No. If I weren't running for office, none of this would have happened."

"We always knew there were risks, Marilyn. And we took them."

She stared at her for a moment. "I suppose. How are you?"

"Oh, I've had better days, weeks…" Alice gave a little chuckle.

She crossed the room and sat beside her. "I understand."

Alice reached for her hand and grasped it. They sat there for several minutes, simply holding hands, saying nothing. To be honest, Alice wasn't sure how to start the conversation.

"I suppose I need to drop out of the race," Marilyn finally said.

She studied her profile. "Is that what you want?"

"Of course not. But it may come to that."

"It's your decision, Marilyn."

She looked at Alice. "I'm really more concerned about you right now. Have you talked to George?"

A bit surprised at her empathy, Alice said, "No. I tried calling him and Ella but neither picked up. I'm sure they are both embarrassed."

"He didn't know about the pictures?"

"No. I saw no need. Not with everything else going on." She wished she hadn't opened up that line of dialogue. Right now, she was in no mood to discuss Griff and other issues.

Marilyn glanced off again, and Alice sighed in relief.

"I still don't know how they got those pictures at Buxton," Marilyn said. "There was barely anyone around."

She didn't know either—but that wasn't the issue. They did, and now here they were.

"Jonathan left me," Marilyn whispered then, staring across the room.

"Because of the pictures?"

"No, he knew about them, but that's not why he left. He accused me of having a fling with Matt, which is totally out of line. He's just a kid, and I would never..." She paused, looking at Alice now. "Jonathan is a bit gun-shy after finding out about you, and then there are my past indiscretions, which we don't even need to go into because that's moot by now."

"He left because of Matt?"

Marilyn huffed a sigh. "Not really. He manufactured that as an excuse. He had the Texas job offer, which was a reason to go. I imagine he was simply tired of playing second fiddle to everything else in my life."

Alice understood.

Marilyn searched her eyes. "You get that, I suppose."

"I do."

"I'm sorry. I guess I'm just better off alone."

That was likely a true statement. Alice looked down at their clasped hands and caressed the back of Marilyn's knuckles. "You're driven, Marilyn. You have goals. And that is okay. Maybe you just need to learn how to let a partner fully share in all that—if a partner is what you truly want. Maybe... You should learn how to live in just one world, and not two or more."

She held her gaze. "I've separated myself like that since I was a kid. Ever since my parents divorced. I had to live in my mom's world one way, and in my dad's another. The only thing that crossed over between them was my need for their attention and affection—which I rarely got. I'm not sure I know how to *not* live like that."

"You can only drive in multiple lanes for so long. Sooner or later, you need to pick one and stay in it."

It occurred to her then that *that* was exactly what *she* should do, as well. *Pick a lane, Alice. And live your life.*

Funny how those nuggets of truth appear on a whim.

A slow, lazy smile broke across Marilyn's face. "I've always loved your compassion, how you looked out for others, freely gave your words of advice, and gave of yourself. And that gem you just said? Is so like you…and so very true. I need to do just that, if I can."

Maggie jumped up from her perch in front of the television, shifting Alice's attention. "We've got breaking news."

Alice rose quickly, and she and Marilyn moved closer to the television.

Maggie knocked on the sliding glass door, signaling Lia. Then, she hustled to the kitchen door and shouted from the back porch to Julia, who was still talking with the officer.

"What's going on?" Alice settled into the sofa. Lia sat on one side of her, Marilyn on the other.

"A banner rolled across the bottom of the screen a few seconds ago saying breaking news in ten minutes." Maggie adjusted the sound.

The kitchen door squeaked as Julia joined them. Out of breath, she sat on the sofa arm. "I'm too wound up to sit for long."

Cheering from a game show sounded from the T.V., then a commercial. Then, a woman sitting behind a news desk….

"We're following breaking news this morning regarding the Marilyn Morgan scandal, and the article and pictures released this morning on *Slant Politics*. As you know, Ms. Morgan is running for the open State Senate position on the Democratic ticket. We're going live to downtown Tuckaway Bay for some perspectives on the ground with Connie Brewster reporting. Connie?"

The scene shifted to the downtown park and gazebo area, the reporter, and several townspeople milling about.

"Yes, Elaine. As you know, Marilyn Morgan was mayor of Tuckaway Bay for three years and recently resigned to focus on her senatorial campaign. Her assistant, Alice McBain, reportedly her lover, also left city government to run Ms. Morgan's campaign." The reporter turned, and the camera moved to a man standing nearby. "I'm here today to get reactions from locals, and David Callahan, who formally worked for the city government, now the communications director for the Fred Faust campaign, has agreed to a few questions. David? I think you know Marilyn and Alice. What is the official reaction from the Faust headquarters?"

"Shit." Marilyn hissed.

David looked into the camera. "We're shocked and appalled, of course. I always felt they were both outstanding and upstanding citizens of Tuckaway Bay—but considering these recent events, the campaign now questions the ethics and morals behind their decisions, and we are even more determined to win the Senate seat for all North Carolinians."

The reporter slanted the mic toward herself. "You have concerns for how she would govern?"

Callahan looked directly at the camera. "We have concerns that she is not the role model for our children, and that her liberal views are not in the best interest of our state."

"How so?"

Callahan laughed. "Have you seen the pictures? *All* of the *intimate* pictures?" He stared again at the camera.

Alice gasped. "What in the world?"

"You slimy cocksucking bastard." Marilyn shot up and started pacing again. "He's making shit up. There is no way there are intimate pictures of us. Absolutely no fucking way."

Julia joined her. "I'm sure you're right, Marilyn. He's spinning."

The reporter chattered on, but Alice heard nothing but the ringing in her ears, until she realized the woman was standing in front of Griff's Grinds, and she pointed the microphone at Griff.

"Oh, shit. Griff."

Lia put her arm around Alice.

"So, I understand you know Alice McBain personally," the reporter asked him. "Have you spoken with her today?"

Griff's expression was deadpan, serious.

Alice's stomach lurched.

"Yes, I know Alice,' he said. "She's a regular here at my coffee shop."

"A regular. Humph," Lia said.

Alice shot her a look.

Griff continued. "Alice McBain is a wonderful person, a hard worker, and a good friend. No, I haven't spoken with her. That's all I have to say."

A breath whooshed from Alice's lungs, and she collapsed against the sofa back. "Good ol' Griff."

Lia leaned in. "I like him better now."

The reporter faced the camera. "This is Connie Brewster reporting on mixed messages coming from Tuckaway Bay. Back to you, Elaine."

Maggie hit the off button on the remote control.

Marilyn stepped up to the group. "Well, it's time to nip this in the bud."

"How so?" Julia asked

"The only way to stop this is to give them what they want."

Alice wasn't sure that was the right approach. "What do you mean, Marilyn?"

She exhaled. "Tell the news crews outside that there will be a press conference downtown at noon, at the campaign headquarters. That should draw them away from here."

Alice turned to her. "Are you sure? Do you want me with you?"

"I am sure, and that's up to you."

Alice looked to Julia for advice and realized none was coming. She was on her own, and that was okay. For all the advice Julia had given her in the past, Alice knew that these next decisions were all on her.

She faced Marilyn and took her hands in hers. "I don't need to be there, Marilyn. You can speak for me, and I'll support you, whatever you say, and in whatever way I can."

Marilyn smiled, her eyes growing a little misty. "I'm better with you not watching me, anyway."

She gripped her hands tighter. "What will you tell them?"

"That I've picked my lane."

Alice knew then, with absolute certainty, that she and Marilyn were over.

<hr>

A FEW MINUTES AFTER THE NOON NEWS STARTED, THE station broke into the press conference feed from Tuckaway Bay.

The camera's lens focused on Marilyn as she stepped up to the microphone on the sidewalk outside of the Morgan campaign headquarters. Matt stood slightly behind her. Two uniformed Tuckaway Bay police officers flanked her on either side.

Lia, Julia, Maggie, and Alice watched from the great room at Tequila Sunrise.

Marilyn began. "Good day. I'll get right to it."

She had no notes, and Alice realized she was going to speak from the heart—which always served her well. It suddenly seemed odd to be watching her from afar, and not there beside her—but that was for the best.

"I could stand here this afternoon," she continued, "and tell you a lie about the pictures you've likely seen on the *Slant Politics* blog today. It wouldn't be unusual for a political candidate to lie to their potential constituents, their comrades in government, or to the general public—but I'm not going to do that. The information that came out earlier today about my love affair with Alice McBain is true."

Alice blew out a breath and stayed focused on the T.V. screen.

"We, meaning my staff and I, considered a spin on the story. Best friends for years. Artificial intelligence images. Fake news. And believe me, I know how to spin a story to my advantage, and it wouldn't be the first time. I know that perception is often reality, and I also know that spinning this story was to no one's advantage.

"But a picture is a thousand words, they say, and let's just talk about those pictures for a moment, and what they might say. I could flash every one of them for you to see, and they would only represent one thing. Love. Neither Alice, nor I, want to sully their beauty, or the beauty of our relationship, by lying about the truth behind them.

"Alice McBain and I were together for over fourteen years. The relationship was grounded in our love for each other. While that relationship has now ended, the fact remains that we were together because we were, simply, in love."

Lia hugged Alice from the side. Maggie stroked her hand.

"Was it wrong in the eyes of our society? Because we were both married, yes.

"Did we cheat on our husbands? Yes, we did.

"Did our husbands know that Alice and I were together, and that we wanted to someday be a couple? Not at first, but they both knew long before those images hit your inboxes this morning."

She hesitated, glancing over the near-silent and growing crowd. "The bottom line is this—those images were private. They were us, our relationship, and someone decided to interfere in our private lives for their personal gain. That will be dealt with in time. You can speculate who that someone might be. The pictures should never have been taken, or posted. They represented a precious moment in time that was stolen from us. Sharing them publicly was an intrusion into our lives. Alice and I never aired our private lives in public."

Again, Marilyn paused, her gaze rolling over the people.

"Several weeks ago, we were approached by two men holding positions in the Tuckaway Bay city government, one of whom now works for Fred Faust, with a proposition. These men intimidated Alice and eliminated her position in the city organizational structure. Essentially, she was fired from a job she'd held for seven years—a job that she excelled at—with no cause for dismissal. These same men blackmailed me and forced my resignation as mayor of this beautiful small town, using the pictures as their weapon. I was to resign or they would post. And rather than let anyone intrude on our personal lives, I resigned. Their motive for this?"

She scanned the crowd as if looking for someone in particular.

"Their motive was to ruin our reputations here, in Tuckaway Bay, where we live. Their goal was to destroy your voter confidence in what I can do for you in the Senate. Basically, they were attempting to eliminate my base voters, causing confusion and chaos, so they could step in and tell you how naughty we have been.

"Well, I'm here to tell you that *will not work.*

"This is an ugly game, and I'm prepared to fight the ugliest of the ugly. I'm not proud of the fact that Alice and I hid our love from the rest of the world for a very long time. We didn't do it because of the stigma of being gay, or bisexual, or for any number of other LGBTQ+ concerns—although that could have easily been a reason. I wanted to keep our relationship secret to protect my career goals, as selfish as that may sound. I knew if we came out anytime over the past dozen years, my political career would suffer, and I didn't want to risk that.

"Alice kept quiet not for me, but to protect her family—a husband she adores, and a daughter she loves to no end. Alice and her husband kept quiet so they could raise their daughter together, amicably, until it was time to let go.

"That was a beautiful sacrifice, and I love her for it. I will *forever* love her for it.

She hesitated before moving on, looking down, and taking a second to gather herself, it seemed to Alice. She, herself, took a steady intake of breath and swiped away a tear or two.

"Now, to answer the question you've all been waiting to ask. Am I dropping out of the race?"

She stared straight ahead, pausing, waiting. Alice smiled. Marilyn always knew how to up the drama. "But before I go there... Someone recently gave me some advice, really good advice—that sometimes you have to pick a lane and stay in it. And with that in mind, I will tell you now that *that's* exactly what I am going to do. Will I drop out of the race?

"Hell no. I picked this Senate lane a long time ago. My dirty laundry is out there—there is nothing else. You decide. And let me be very clear—my dirty laundry is that I cheated on my husband—not that I am gay. I am a proud member of the LGBTQ+ community and will make that known from this day forward.

"I am in my lane. I'm staying there until the end. I'll not be intimidated or blackmailed or cajoled to quit. I will fight for *all* the rights of *all* people—and that includes the right to privacy...and the right to love *how* you wish, *who* you wish, and *when* you wish, openly and authentically. With no need to hide from anyone."

The crowd erupted with shouts and applause. Marilyn smiled and briefly waved, then ducked back into the headquarters.

Matt stepped up to the microphone. "I have four minutes for questions."

The picture faded. Alice picked up the remote control and turned off the television. "Well." She exhaled long and looked at her friends.

"That was good," Maggie said.

"Brilliant, actually." Julia rose and stepped to look out over the deck. "The news crowd is thinning down on the beach. I think you're officially old news, Alice."

"Thank, God."

Julia's phone buzzed then and they all looked her way. "Hello?" She paused, listening. "That's fine. Send her up."

Alice blinked. "Who is it? Marilyn? How did she get here so quickly?"

"It's not Marilyn." Julia headed for the kitchen door and opened it.

"Then who?"

Ella came rushing inside. "Mom! Mom!"

Alice ran to her. "Oh sweetheart. Are you okay? Where's your dad?"

"He's at the house." Ella's tears were almost Alice's undoing. "I'm fine. But, oh my God, Mom. I feel so bad for you. How could this happen? I want you to know I don't care about the stupid pictures, or that you were in love with Marilyn. I was just... I was so worried. We, Dad and me, *we* were worried, so we came back. Are you sure you're okay?"

Alice wrapped her arms around her daughter and held her tight. "At this moment, I'm perfectly okay. I love you, sweetheart. Thank you for coming." It meant everything that she had her daughter's support.

Ella hugged her so tight she could barely breathe.

Julia ducked back into the great room. "Guess who else I just found?"

Carol, Belle, and Hannah rolled through the back door carrying their beach gear and luggage, tossing everything into a pile on the kitchen floor. "Surprise! We're early!"

Twenty-One

Having the younger girls at beach week was the perfect distraction for Alice. The energy in the house was different—upbeat, carefree, and animated. Not that her girlfriends weren't, at times, all three. With the younger generation, it was just—different.

They ordered dinner in last evening—BBQ, coleslaw, sweet corn, and country biscuits—and then stayed up way too late on the deck chatting. While the girls were still sleeping in that morning, the older set was up and drifting into the day.

Apparently, Alice wasn't the only one who felt the energy.

"Last night with the girls was nice. Wasn't it? I didn't realize Hannah had such a sense of humor," Lia said.

"And Belle?" Julia added. "Her energy amazes me. I can't imagine all she does in a day, and with a baby."

"She's a super big help to me," Lia said. "I'm sure she's missing baby Grace right now, though."

"But it's a good break for her. I'm glad she could get away."

"I'm just happy that Ella and Carol are getting along." Alice chuckled.

"I'll second that! It's nice having them here. Good idea, Julia." Maggie poked at a leftover doughnut from Duck Donuts. "I seriously

197

cannot believe this doughnut is still here from yesterday. Why someone hasn't eaten it by now, I'll never know." She took a healthy bite of the caramel and bacon-covered confection.

Julia drank the rest of her coffee and poured another cup. "I can't believe we have only two more days, and then beach week is over for another year."

"Having the girls here reminds me of when we were their age." Lia popped a couple of slices of bread into the toaster. "Wait. We *were* their age the first time we came here. Right?"

"We were in college, so just about," Maggie added. "They sleep late, like we did, too."

Julia poured another cup. "Youth. But damn, what a week this has been already."

"Tell me about it." Alice grimaced. "Ranks right up there with the all-time worst weeks of my life."

"Oh, Alice," Lia said. "Have you heard from Marilyn?"

She hadn't and doubted she would. "No. And it's okay. I feel like we left things with an understanding. Sort of." She settled into a chair at the table. "It's time for us to part ways."

Lia brought her toast and coffee to the table, too. "You don't have to talk about it."

"It's okay. *I'm* okay. I've come to realize something."

At her words, Julia and Maggie joined them.

"What's that?" Maggie said.

She hesitated for a moment, staring into her cup. "There are a couple of conversations I need to have, with Ella and with George, and then I can move forward. Marilyn's honesty yesterday was bold, and I need to be just as bold. I've lived in the shadows for most of my adult life. It's time for me to step out of the dim, and into the bright. It's time for me to live the life of my choosing, rather than the life others expected of me."

They were silent for a heartbeat or two. "Will you stay here?" Lia asked.

"I have no reason to move." She studied their faces and realized they were concerned. "I'm not going anywhere, you all! And please don't worry. There is absolutely nothing that could change our relationship. At least in my eyes." She smirked. "Unless you kick me out?"

"Well, that's not happening," Lia said. "Seriously, Alice.

"I concur." Julia slapped the table and stood. "Well. I need to call Sam. I feel like I haven't talked to him in days."

Lia got up, too. "And I should check in with Zach. With both Belle and me gone from the resort, I worry about what kinds of decisions that man will make!"

Julia and Lia skittered off.

Maggie rose and reached for Alice's hand. "Take a walk with me?"

Alice glanced up and took her hand, somewhat surprised Maggie asked her. "Of course."

They left the house and headed for the surf, walking along that narrow juncture of sand and sea. "That sun is going to get hot before we know it." Alice kicked at the waves spilling over her bare toes. "I hope our girls don't get burned this afternoon on the beach."

"Me, too. But the morning is still pretty. Look," she pointed out to sea. "The waves cresting way out look like shining diamonds in the sun."

Alice found the sparkles and laughed. "They do, don't they?"

They walked a few feet further, hand in hand. "You seem happy, Alice."

"I feel relieved, and honestly, free."

Maggie stopped and turned toward her. "Isn't that such a wonderful feeling? It took me a minute after Max died to get there, but when I did... It was awesome."

Alice understood that. "I'm sure every day is going to be better than the last one."

"It will be. I'm just so happy for you." She reached into her dress pocket. "I have something. You can keep it or pass it along. It's up to you."

"What in the world?"

Maggie tucked the heart-shaped rock Alice had found the other day into her palm. "I painted it for you," she said.

And it is beautiful. "Oh, Maggie. It's lovely." The colors of a Tuckaway Bay sunrise spilled over the rock, with streaks of yellow and peach and lavender and blue. In darker shades of rose and purple, Maggie had painted the words *I Wish You Love* across the top.

Maggie curled Alice's fingers around the rock. "Whatever path your life takes you, I want you to know, that the one thing I wish for you, my friend, is love." She kissed her cheek. "I want you to find the love of your life, Alice. You deserve that."

"As do you, Maggie." She could barely see the rock because of her tears. Alice clasped the stone firmly against her chest, then pulled Maggie in closer for a tight hug. "Thank you, my friend. I love you."

<hr>

THEY SEPARATED, AND ALICE WATCHED MAGGIE'S GAZE drift off behind her, toward Tequila Sunrise. "I'm heading back to the house now," she told Alice.

"Sure." Turning as Maggie strolled away, she noticed Ella coming toward her. She slipped the rock into her pocket. "I didn't think you'd be up for a while."

Ella grinned and gave her a hug. "I came down as you were leaving with Maggie. Can I walk with you?"

"Of course."

They wandered for a while, dodging seagulls and ghost crabs and the ripples of a rising tide, picking at shell fragments and other dead sea life along the way.

"Mom, do you remember when I was little, and Grandma and Grandpa had that fishing shack down the beach? Before they developed that area? Sometimes, you and Dad and I would stay there just so we could get up early and go shelling."

The memory warmed her heart. It was one of her favorites. "I do. You remember my rule?"

Ella laughed. "Of course! I had to be up and ready to go, whenever *you* were going on your early morning beach walk. You would not wake me or wait for me to get dressed."

"That's right." She remembered the summer of Ella's long, skinny legs and the blue-and-white bathing suit she wore until the seat ripped. "And did I ever leave without you?"

"Just once, as I recall."

"And you never made me wait again."

Ella hooked her arm with hers. "Those were good days."

"Yes," Alice nodded. "And there will be more good days. Just different."

They walked arm-in-arm for a while longer.

"Mom. I want you to know… I'm okay with you being gay. It was hard at first, I think because it was so unexpected coming from Carol, and it hurt that you and Dad kept it from me for so long. But I've had time to think about it, and you were right in doing that."

Alice paused her steps, facing Ella. She cupped her daughter's cheeks in her hands. "Oh, sweetheart," she whispered. "I'm so sorry for all your heartache, and for all the mistakes I made that affected you."

Ella shook her head. "No, don't be sorry. It was growing pains, for you and for all of us. We've had to stretch in ways we never expected, but it is all good. You know?"

"You're sure?" Alice's eyes felt misty.

"I'm sure. I want you to be happy, Mom. And I want us to be best friends again."

Those words nearly cracked her heart wide open. "Oh, Ella," she whispered. "I want that, too."

Alice caught her up in a warm, tight embrace, and exhaled deeply. She wasn't sure she ever wanted to let her girl go.

"You should talk to him, Mom." Ella spoke softly.

Alice pulled back, gazing into her eyes. "Your dad?"

"Who else?"

Good question, of course. But Ella didn't know about Griff, or so she thought, anyway, so she wouldn't have meant anyone other than George.

"I want to, sweetheart. Very much. I don't know if he is ready, though. Or if he wants to talk to me."

Ella hesitated. "He… He still loves you, Mom."

She swallowed a lump in her throat. "I'm not so sure, Ella."

"He told me he's forgiven you. He loved our life together, the three of us. Please give him a chance to say that. Will you?"

Of course, she could do that. "I think I should wait for him to reach out to me. What do you think?"

Ella shook her head. "No. He wants you to come to him. He wants to know you still care."

That almost broke her heart. She would always care, and she couldn't bear the thought of George thinking she didn't.

"Sweetheart, I want you to know something. I will always love your Dad, but I do not want to send the wrong message to you, or to him. I'll reach out. Today. But know that things may not turn out as you want."

Ella hugged her. "Mom. All I want is for you to be happy. And for dad to be happy. That's all I ever want. Whatever you choose."

"Even if we can't be happy together?"

"Even if."

They both turned as shouts erupted from the beach house deck. Hannah, Belle, and Carol waved and called out for Ella.

"We're heading to Nags Head," Ella told her. "I'm going to go with them. See you later this evening for dinner."

"Yes. We have reservations at the crab house." Alice smiled. "Have fun, honey. I love you."

"I love you too, Mom."

She watched her go, then pulled out her cell phone and sent George a text message.

Alice: *Meet me at Quigley Pier in thirty?*

George: *Already there. Meet you halfway.*

Alice supposed that was all she could ask of him, or anyone.

SHE SPOTTED GEORGE A FEW MINUTES LATER, SAUNTERING toward her. She'd know his physique anywhere—tall, not too thin, but not too husky, either. Ella got her long legs from him.

He wore that fishing sun hat she'd always thought looked dorky on him—but he loved it. Laughing a little to herself, she realized how much she had enjoyed living with this man over the years, and how much she was going to miss him.

As he drew closer, she could see the concern on his face, and when he stopped in front of her, the kindness in his eyes.

"Rough day yesterday?"

She nodded. "I survived."

"Like a trooper, I'm sure."

"George," she began. "I'm so sorry for what all this means for you. I should have told you about the pictures."

He shrugged. "Seriously, Alice, would it have made a difference? I wouldn't have been blindsided publicly, but the overall effect would be the same."

She supposed that was true. "I hate that. It must feel humiliating. I mean, I feel it, but it's probably worse for you. Will this be difficult at school? Middle schoolers can be terrible."

He glanced off toward the ocean. "I took another job near Ella, Alice. I'm moving."

To be honest, she was relieved for him. "That is probably a good thing."

He met her gaze. "Come with me. Let's start over."

It wasn't a question, but a very clear statement of what he wanted. She shook her head, looking at the sand. The saltwater flowed in and out over their toes, erasing their footprints. Erasing their history. "I can't, George. I hope you understand."

"Alice." He grasped her hands and tugged her closer. "I forgive you. We can start over. Let's try again. I... I'm not sure I know how to do this without you."

"George. I can't." She held his gaze, her vision blurry with tears. "The good part is, we don't have to do it alone—navigating this new chapter of our lives—if we remain friends."

"Friends."

"We've shared a lifetime and a child. We may not be lovers any longer, but perhaps what we can have, is stronger than that."

"Perhaps." The look on his face wasn't convincing.

"George... I want you to be okay. I want you to live a full life. I want you to find love again."

He huffed out a breath and shook his head. "I can't even think about falling in love again."

She lifted the heart-shaped rock from her pocket and placed it in his palm, much like Maggie had done earlier for her. "Maggie painted this and gave it to me earlier today. Now I'm giving it to you."

"Why?"

"We can't be together, George, not like we once were, although I will always, always love you. I've been caught between two worlds for a very long time. I need to explore who I am, what I need, and how I want to live the rest of my days. I want to love again, genuinely. And thanks to you, I know how to do that." She searched his eyes.

"Because of what we had, George, I know what true love is. And because of Ella, and *for* Ella, I will always *want* you in my life."

She edged closer and leaned up to kiss him on his cheek. "I choose to keep you, George McBain. Can you live with that?"

He touched his forehead to hers. "I will always want you in my life, Alice. How can I refuse?"

She smiled. "I love you, George, for everything you were to me, and still are to me. Most of all, I love you because you love us, Ella and me, so very much. But I also want to set you free, so you can find love again."

George swiped at his eyes and pulled her closer, wrapping his arms snug around her. She felt his warmth, his compassion, his love... But most of all she felt the soft kiss he placed on top of her head, as he'd done countless times before.

She'd needed that simple gesture.

And he knew that.

"I hope you can live with that," she whispered. "I want you to soar. To take this time to live your best life, too." Leaning back, she searched his eyes. "I wish us both love."

Epilogue

November, Day of the Election

ALICE SWITCHED OFF THE TELEVISION AND YAWNED. SHE'D stayed up too late and had an early morning. Yawning, she headed for the stairs, turning off lights as she went.

Her phone buzzed and she watched the text messages roll in.

Julia: *Well, she did it*

Lia: *I told you she would!*

Julia: *I'm so relieved. Faust is a lunatic.*

Maggie: *What's going on?*

Julia: *The election, Maggie! Marilyn won.*

Maggie: *Oh good. We don't need that nutcase.*

Alice finally had to laugh and added to the conversation

Alice: *It's exciting.*

Lia: *Have you heard from her?*

Alice: *No. I don't expect to.*

Lia: *I thought just maybe.*

Alice held no expectations that she would ever hear from Marilyn. That ship had sailed, and it was okay.

Alice: *I'm fine. It's all good.*

Maggie: *I'm going back to sleep now. Nite.*

Lia: *Oh, just a reminder. Baby Grace's birthday party is on Christmas Eve. Put it on your calendars, please!*

Julia: *Are you sure, Lia? I mean, after last year....*

Lia: *Seriously? Where else would you want to be over the holidays than Sea Glass Inn?*

Thank You!

Thank you for reading *I Wish You Love*.

Alice's story has been building for a while in the Tuckaway Bay series. The one thing I wanted for Alice, was for her to recognize herself as important—in her own life, and in the lives of others. I wanted her to grow into her own person and frankly, get out from under Marilyn's thumb. While I do think she and Marilyn had a loving relationship, it was definitely one-sided.

I also couldn't leave George hanging. We know his future is uncertain, too. But I hope I left you with a satisfying ending for both George and Alice, with lots of hope for their futures.

Love, Madeleine

If you would like to leave a review at your favorite bookstore, or at my website, I would be most appreciative. I look forward to, and thank you for, your honest opinion.

You can leave your review here: https://maddiejamesbooks.com/products/i-wish-you-love-alices-story

Anywhere But Here

WREN AND WILLOW

When women become too powerful, someone always wants to silence them.

Twin sisters Wren and Willow Harper have built an empire on secrets —political scandals, high-powered affairs, and the kind of leverage that topples careers. They know all the powerful people, and their covert indiscretions. They're savvy, fearless, and untouchable... Until they're not.

Someone wants them gone.

Their only option is to abandon their empire and run.

Forced into hiding, the Harper twins vanish without a trace. But staying hidden proves harder than they imagined when danger follows. Even under witness protection, they do not feel safe. With nowhere else to go, they return to the last place they ever expected to seek refuge: Tuckaway Bay.

Back in the town they once fled, Wren and Willow must decide if hiding in plain sight among old friends is their best chance at survival —or the biggest risk of all.

Anywhere But Here is a powerful story of sisterhood, survival, and what happens when women refuse to stay silent.

Learn more: https://maddiejamesbooks.com/products/anywhere-but-here

More Tuckaway Bay

Beach Therapy: A Novel
The Space in Between: Julia's Story
The Christmas Storm
The Me I Left Behind: Maggie's Story
I Wish You Love: Alice's Story (August 2025)
Anywhere But Here: Wren & Willow (May 2026)

...and more to come.

About Madeleine Jaimes

Madeleine Jaimes (aka Maddie James) is a contemporary women's fiction author whose emotionally charged novels explore the real-life social issues affecting women today. Her stories reflect powerful themes like addiction and recovery, domestic violence, LGBTQ+ identity, and family struggles. Her characters remind us that healing is never linear—and that strength comes in many forms.

She believes the most important stories we tell are the ones we whisper to ourselves.

Set against emotionally rich backdrops, Madeleine's stories invite readers to pause, reflect, and feel seen. Her popular *Tuckaway Bay* series reflects her passion for writing layered characters and small-town stories where every woman's journey matters.

Learn more at www.maddiejamesbooks.com.

Want Insider News?

Be the first to get the latest news about Maddie James Books, no matter the pen name! Get new release news, free ebooks, sales and discounts, sneak peeks, and exclusive content! Just add your email address at this link, https://maddiejamesbooks.com/pages/newsletter and we'll take it from there!